Hey Mary

by George Banworth

This book is available from:
The 101 Foundation, Inc.
P.O. Box 151
Asbury, NJ 08802-0151
Phone: 908-689 8792
Fax: 908-689 1957
www.101foundation.com
email: 101@101foundation.com

1st printing, May, 2002 — 10,000 copies
Printed in the U.S.A.
by
The 101 Foundation, Inc.
edited by Dr. Rosalie A. Turton

ISBN: 1-890137-58-8

Dedicated to the Love of my Life,
Mary Immaculate Ever Virgin.
She is so beautiful because She loves.
May we learn from Her to love each other well
and thus become beautiful like Her.

Table of Contents:

Cover art by Sister M. Ambrosine, A.C.C.

The Story Behind the Painting

(After a Peace Conference where this painting of Mary was shown, because of many requests we asked Sister Ambrosine for the story behind it. She hesitated to give it to us, because she wants Our Lady to be known and not herself, but finally, she reluctantly wrote the following:)

The first day in Medjugorje, I attended an early morning Mass. I told Our Dear Lord and Mary, "I am here, but why?" Not long afterwards, the thought came to me...*make a retreat out of these days here.* I informed my group of the decision, and spent time at the Church watching and meeting people from all over the world, praying, hearing a talk in English every afternoon, and above all... curiously watching small groups of 10 to 20 people go into one of the sacristies daily.

When Mass was offered at the main altar in the Church, a sister would lock the door to that sacristy. One afternoon when a group came out of this special sacristy, I suddenly rose and slowly walked toward the door and went in. The room was small...a few chairs around the walls, an altar, a large Crucifix behind it on the wall, and in one corner to the left of the altar was one of the ugliest statues I have ever seen of Mary, *or so I thought.*

I felt that the lines, the mass, the color all lacked the beauty any art piece should convey to the beholder! But, on second thought, I realized the peasant artisan who made it perhaps caught something Mary wanted to convey to the world...let go of the externals...internal joy and peace are what truly counts, and *these he caught!*

As I sat there, I began to let the Holy Spirit take over in me as I went into contemplative prayer. I just closed my eyes and asked the Holy Spirit to take me deep down into my inner self, and there, in the presence of the Holy Trinity, just BE...asking the Holy Spirit to heal me of all that needed to be healed.

About ten minutes later, I slowly started to say the *Our Father*, and when I came to the last phrase, I gradually opened my eyes on the words, "...for Thine is the Kingdom, the Power, and the Glory." And, then I beheld, to my utter amazement, not the old ugly statue, but a living and most beautiful young woman, about twenty years old, in place of the old statue...yet it seemed within the lines of the statue.

I could hardly believe it, and I tried *not* to close my eyes or even bat my eyelids so that I would not miss anything. She was far more beautiful than any young woman I had ever seen, (and being in the theater and having studied in New York city, traveled in Paris, London, Rome, Madrid, etc., I have seen some of the world's, so called, most beautiful women). But, *they* were *nothing* in comparison!

Her eyes spoke. She did not need words. Her look encompassed the whole world; it seemed as if She looked far beyond me, beyond Medjugorje, etc. Her skin was young, most beautiful...flushed and radiant with a rosy-like healthy color. Her one hand extended out, as if to say, "Come; be not afraid. I bring what you all want...*peace*." She did not move forward, but somehow indicated, as She seemed to lean forward, that She *would* come, if invited.

As I sat there, She said so much in prefect silence and stillness...enough, that it has changed my whole life. Her lips were pursed as if She wanted to speak, waiting for someone else to finish speaking. I did not pay much attention to Her clothes. I focused only on Her face.

During all this time, which seemed perhaps longer than it was, I did not want to close my eyes for an instant, for fear that I would lose Her. But finally, I had to do so, since my eyes hurt a little and seemed dry...so, I went back into contemplative prayer. As I came out of it again with the *Our Father*, I opened my eyes, hoping once more to see Her...but She was gone, and there again was the old statue.

Early in the 1990's, I felt the urge to paint Mary as I saw Her. I had never painted a portrait and I had never had art lessons, and had only painted scenery in my retirement. One day, I felt the urge so strongly, I sketched Mary and then painted the portrait.

The greatest artist in the world would be unable to capture the love and beauty that I saw that afternoon, but I share this poor effort with you in the hope of giving you a vague idea of the love and wonder of Mary.

Chapter 1

Why Didn't It Turn Gold?

Late in 1989, out of the blue, a woman walked up to me and said, "Have you heard what is going on in Medjugorje, a little town in Yugoslavia? The Blessed Mother is appearing there." I said, "Yes, I am aware of that. I read about it in a paper regarding a Marian Conference in Pittsburgh." She went on to say, "There is a tour group being arranged to go there and I want to go there and I was wondering if you would like to go there too." Well, I wasn't ready for that so I told her, "No, I don't think so. Besides I already believe in the Blessed Mother. That isn't important for me." She said, "I would really be interested in the experience. Why don't you think about it?" I said, "OK."

Two weeks later she asked again, and I said, "No, I don't think I want to go at this time." And, then she said, "Why don't you give me a Rosary. I will take your Rosary along and I will have the Blessed Mother bless your Rosary. I am taking everybody's Rosary." I said, "Well, I do not have a Rosary with me but the next time I will bring a Rosary along." I was at this location every week.

So, two weeks went by. I took a Rosary along, and she took this Rosary and put it in a little paper bag about two inches wide and about four inches deep and folded it up and dropped it in her purse, along with maybe six to eight others. So, now after a few more weeks, here comes this lady back. She has all these Rosaries left. She never took them out of the bags they were in and gave everybody their Rosary back. I took mine out of the bag and I didn't see anything different, but one thing I did notice was that everyone else's Rosary either was gold or had turned gold, and mine was the only one that remained silver.

To say that I was stunned, well that was putting it mildly. I was somewhat embarrassed. Of course, I was aware of my Rosary. Nobody else was but I thought, "How could you take that Rosary in the bottom of that purse, inside of that paper bag, and keep it separated from the rest, and have every Rosary change but mine. How is it possible? You had to really pay close attention and you must have really wanted very much to bring that Rosary back to me like it was to show me that everyone else's had turned gold."

And, I will say I was hurt. I really became quite upset and I then talked directly to Her. I said, "If you can pay that much attention to that little Rosary inside that paper bag, inside that purse, you must have an idea what is going on in my life. You must be paying very close attention, and I want to tell you that I am not very happy with what you did. I think what you did was not a very nice thing to do."

I really couldn't get it out of my mind. I mean it was so overpowering to me that there was not anything else that I could think about. The more I thought about it, the more I became very unhappy, to the point where I really became angry with Our Lady. I thought I had Her attention, so I would talk to Her basically all day long. For days this was going on. I am really telling Her off and really complaining, and then I thought, "Well, maybe You can make up for it. You can still change the Rosary to gold."

Now I put the Rosary on my night stand and I left it there. I wasn't using it. I wasn't very much into the Rosary. I was never away from the faith. I always made Mass every Sunday, but that was about it. And, my life-style was such, that I was into the things of the world. It really took up all of my day. I was very busy. I was traveling a lot. Business was, I felt, a necessity in my life. It was to me most important. But I could not get the Rosary off my mind and it was the Blessed Mother that I thought about all day long. I was very upset with Her and I finally told Her, "Hey, Mary, You can make up for this. You can still change that Rosary to gold."

I thought about it to the point where I actually felt, "Yeah, if I think about it hard enough, I think She probably will." So I kept thinking about it. And, every day I would say, "OK...now today would be a pretty good day. I think today should be the day for You to do this." And, time goes by, I think 2 months go by, and I finally thought, "This has gone on long enough. I think You had better turn that Rosary to gold. In fact, I'll give You until 5 o'clock tonight. At that time, when I get home, I expect that Rosary to be gold."

That evening, when I got home, I went directly to the Rosary and there it was, just like it was before. Nothing happened. And, I said, "Hey,

Mary, why did You single me out?" I think, at this time, I had a total meltdown. I realized Our Lady was not at fault; I was. I was not worthy of anything. I now realize that it wasn't Her attention I had...I had that all of the time. Now She had my attention. I was not a model person. I was totally worldly and I now realized I was headed for Hell.

My life needed a new focus. I came up with another idea, all new. I wanted Mary to visit me. Why not? I told Her, "You give up to 10 minutes every day to six visionaries each. I just want You for one time for 30 seconds." Not a big request, I thought. I felt this really could happen, and then I realized I wasn't ready. I said, "Hey, Mary, wait until I go to confession." I wanted to be more worthy.

I felt small, yet I became aware that I had fallen so deeply in love with this Lady I wanted only Her. I didn't just want to share everything; I literally wanted to give Her every worldly possession I had. She helped me in a most unusual way. I wanted to live as She wanted, and I would now try to be in His Grace, so when Mary came physically to visit me, I would be somewhat ready. I thought every day, "Today could be that day."

I was thinking of Her more than ever. Joy was being left alone so I could think of Her without interruptions. I found myself jealous of Her. I felt the need for a prayer life on a consistent daily basis but I didn't know how to pray. I felt guilty and ashamed. I wanted to be a different person.

Somebody gave me a Novena—something to do with St. Bridget—15 meditations which took about 20 minutes a day. Then I became acquainted with the Divine Mercy Chaplet. And, a couple of months later I started saying the Rosary every day. And then, about a year later, I began an hour a day before the exposed Blessed Sacrament.

On June 22, 1991, I had my first heart attack. It was a Saturday morning. I was so happy during this time—in the emergency room and in the Cat scan room and the whole week in St. Luke's Hospital—because I credited Mary with making me start to turn my life around before this took place. I felt great because I didn't do it out of fear because I was facing death. I just wasn't that thrilled about living anymore anyway. I was thinking more and more about life after death.

I told Mary, "You come and get me, I will gladly go. If You don't come to get me, I'm not going." Mary knew how I meant it. She understood. I wanted Her to approve of me and welcome me, even though I didn't feel worthy. I recovered, and a year later I added another hour a day before the exposed Blessed Sacrament.

By now my legs were so bad I could barely get around. I really didn't care. I was happy to suffer. I felt a joy in offering that up. I had a lot of making up to do. It is now that I began to think about going to Medjugorje. There was a problem though. The war was going on and it prohibited anyone from going there.

Chapter 2

An Encounter With The Sisters

Behold, one day Brother Stephen, a Monk from New Melleray, walked into my office. He has been such a good and close friend for many years. I asked him where he was heading. He told me, after getting the information he needed, he was going to the Trappistines to help them with something, I forget what. I had a newsletter and I asked him if he would deliver it to one of the Sisters for me.

"Sure," he said. "What is this about?" I said that it concerns what we can expect in the economy. I told him I enjoy learning all I can about our local, national, and global economy. He then said, "Why don't you study the prophecies?" I told him, "I'm not aware of them."

He said, "You ought to stop out and talk to Brother Kevin. He has been studying them for over 20 years." I informed him that I definitely would and very soon, you can be sure. Within a couple of days Brother Stephen arranged some time between Brother Kevin and myself. Brother Stephen asked if he could sit in. I didn't know he would even be interested, but I was pleased that he joined us.

We went to a private room, the three of us, and Brother Kevin asked the questions. I was never shy about expressing my opinions. I told him, according to my calculations, when our nation would go broke. The truth is that nations cannot file bankruptcy.

When I finished, Brother Kevin said, "You are probably right on, except, I think you are somewhat early. If you want to know exactly what is going to happen, you need to read three books." I was definitely interested. He gave me one book and the title for the other two. I was now off and running in a new direction. I think I averaged probably two to three books a week after that.

I was also now turning my desire to become involved in a different direction. I wanted to help Our Lady. One day I turned to a Catholic TV program and without knowing anything about what was being shown, I decided, "Now that would be a good cause, but how do you get acquainted with people like that? I'll make a phone call."

A couple weeks later I found myself inside the offices of this TV station in Birmingham. Some construction was going on and a Sister John Paul decided to make use of my help. She had been a contractor and builder before joining the convent and, I will say, her abilities far surpassed mine. She had just completed an addition to the network property: a mail room to handle thousands of pieces of mail almost daily. Downstairs was this huge room. Sister told me, "We would like to finish this so we can receive people by busloads and offer maybe a refreshment and snack, or possibly a homily by one of the guest speakers at the Network, or maybe by one of the Professors at our school, or someone from the men's Monastery."

Next was probably one of the first mysterious happenings I was involved with. Sister John Paul said, "Tables and chairs—how many can we get in here?" I told her that I would measure it out and give her a call in a few days. I counted the ceiling tiles and when I came home, I figured out what I thought would be needed. When I told Sister John Paul, she informed me she thought four more tables and sixteen more chairs than I had come up with. I thought, "Why did you ask me? You already had this figured out."

I needed to come up with tables to match the driftwood wood trim in the room and the wallpaper on the walls. I thought, "Impossible! Where can I find a 42" to 44" square or square round driftwood top table or game table?" No supplier we had offered this, so I called a rep for our largest supplier and asked if he could take a top they had and eliminate the leaf and make it a solid top and make a base for it. It was not what I wanted but it would be the best I could get. The rep said, "I'm going to the factory next week and I'll find out if we can do that." That evening, I went to the chapel and told Mary, "We have a difficult job but it is a good cause. This room is to be used for retreats."

Ten days later, I got a call from the rep at the factory. He said, "Guess what? The factory just inventoried and found 200 tops 42" square with a clipped corner, and wood edge in driftwood. Nobody knows where they came from. They told me they would build a pedestal base and sell it for half price."

I called Sister John Paul and asked if I could place the order sight unseen. I told her, “It is a 42" square round driftwood top, and they will build a pedestal for it and sell it to us at half price.” Sister John Paul replied, “Yes, and it has a wood edge too, doesn't it?” I wondered, exactly what kind of beings am I dealing with here?

Now the chairs they picked out were available from another factory and they told me they could make them up at a very good discount, if I chose one of three fabrics. One of these fabrics was an exact match to the wallpaper. The reason for the discount was, it was an over-run on a job they provided for Hilton Hotels. Forty years in this business did not prepare me for what was going on here... but this was just a prelude.

I had confidence that Mary would carry out anything I suggested, using proper judgment of course, and I realized Her Son could enforce Her every request. In fact, I felt He could not refuse Her.

Some weeks later, I am back at the same place in Birmingham and I am sitting with the Mother Superior. She looked at me, and she said, “George, we need some furniture. Can you help us?”

“OK, what is it?” I said.

“We have this short wave global radio network we are building and we are having a press conference, and there will be many people from around the world and there is no place for anyone to sit down.” I asked, “What do you need?” She said, “We need to furnish the entire building. I'll get you a fax.”

She went to the phone and called the only person at the site. He was an experienced short wave retired Navy veteran. He sent the fax. (A copy of the fax is at the end of this chapter.) You should have seen it. It looked somewhat like this: twelve desks, ten roll around chairs, one computer center, etc. I silently laughed. Then she added, "The press conference is in three weeks."

I thought, "This is Alabama. I'm in Iowa. I'm to furnish a building in three weeks. I don't have a clue what to put in here, and so I told her that on Monday, I would call her from my office and get more information. She said, "No, you can't. I am leaving for Europe tomorrow. You can ask for Inez."

On Monday I called Inez and left a message. Tuesday, I called Inez and left a message. Wednesday I called, but this time I called her personal secretary, Sydney, and I got results. She got Inez and put her on the phone, only to have Inez inform me that she was told I would let her know when everything was ready, and if I wanted to know anything I had to call the Navy Veteran.

Well, I called and after every question I would ask, he would say, "Whatever you do will be just fine." Finally, I said, "Look, I can't furnish anything this way. I don't know any colors or sizes; I don't even know window positions. He then said, "Don't worry, this building has no windows."

He then told me this is a round building, no windows, built on top of a mountain, and the entire building is enclosed in copper. He let me know that he knows nothing about furniture and there are no floors or walls painted so he will be satisfied with whatever I do.

So, I went to the chapel. "Hey Mary, we have 18 days. I'll order and you pick things out, color, size, etc. You need to expedite and follow the shipments and get this all delivered before the press conference. OK?" I am positive something will be delivered; I can handle that. I can't handle what gets delivered. I don't even know where it goes except on top of a mountain about 30 miles out of Birmingham. I let Mary handle everything.

So I called D.M.I. and told them, "I want to order 12 desks and make them executive." They asked, "What kind and size and finish would you like?" I replied, "Well, I don't know, so why don't you send anything you have. Just remember, do it quick. OK?" I ordered everything that way. This was very difficult because companies were very reluctant to ship things this way, but I had all the calls completed in about three days.

After this, I had no contact with anyone, not one supplier, not one trucking company, no radio network, no Top Gun. On the 18th day, the day of the press conference, I kept wondering, "Is something happening today?" Never a word all day.

The next day I couldn't wait any longer. I called and what I thought was a very young man answered the phone. I asked for the old Navy veteran. He said, "Sorry. He is out. Would you like to talk to him on his car phone?" I said, "No. Tell me, did you have a press conference there yesterday?"

"Oh, yes sir," was his reply. I said, "Were there many people?"

"Oh, yes sir," was his reply. Such politeness. He must be another Navy veteran. Then he added, "People from Australia, Korea, China, India, England, all over Europe. From Germany, France, etc." I said, "And, did you have any furniture there?"

"Oh, yes sir," he replied again. I said, "Was the furniture all there?" He then replied, "I have no way of knowing that because I have no way of knowing what is supposed to be here, but I can tell you one thing. Whoever picked this furniture out did a super job." Thank you. End of conversation.

It was like three to four more days before anyone called me. The Top Gun said, "I don't know how you did this. There is not one item in this building that I feel I could take out of here and replace with something better." Naturally! What do you expect? I have the best decorator.

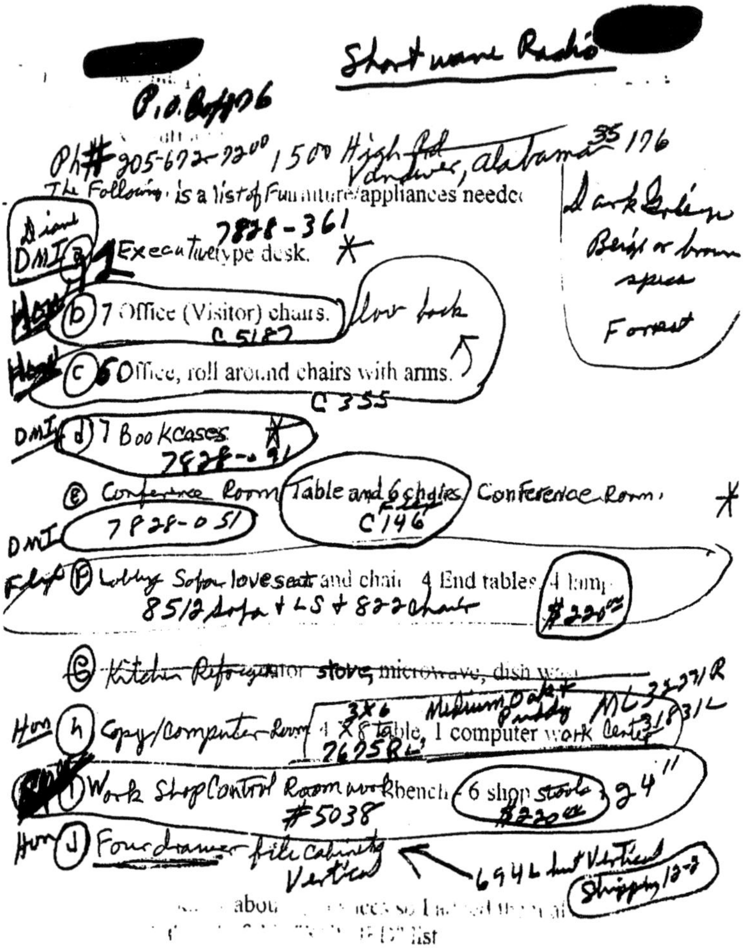
[redacted] Short wave Radio [redacted]

P.O. Box 406

Ph# 205-672-2200 1500 High Rd Vandiver, Alabama 35176

The Following is a list of Furniture/appliances needed

a) Executive type desk. 7828-361 *

b) 7 Office (Visitor) chairs. C5187 love back

c) 6 Office, roll around chairs with arms. C355

d) 7 Bookcases. 7828-091

e) Conference Room Table and 6 chairs Conference Room. C146 7828-051 *

f) Lobby Sofa loveseat and chair 4 End tables 4 lamps 8512 Sofa + LS + 822 chair $220

g) Kitchen Refrigerator stove, microwave, dish wash

h) Copy/Computer Room 4 X 8 table, 1 computer work Center 3x6 2625R Medium Oak + Paddy ML 3227R 3181L

i) Work Shop Control Room workbench 6 shop stools 24" #5038 $220

j) Four drawer file cabinets Vertical 694L but Vertical Shipping 12-7

Dark Cologne Beige or brown specs Forest

(Above: The fax requesting the needed furniture)

Chapter 3

Off To Medjugorje

One day, I received a call from Sister John Paul, who said, "I am asking for help. Our Order is building a convent retreat center complex and I saw the job you did furnishing the Radio Network building. Would you consider helping us with the furnishing of our retreat center, because we know nothing about furniture?" I thought, "Oh, yes you do," but I replied, "Sure, I know that for a project this size, I can save you over a million dollars just by eliminating mistakes. Also, I can protect you from the world, which is not always thinking of the best interests of the Sisters." This project took about five years, with more than daily contact. Many days it was hourly contact.

The job was more than a privilege. I felt it was even more than a blessing. It was a total reward. This entire work was an attempt to please Our Lady. Nothing else mattered. The name of the retreat center is Casa Maria, which means Mary's House.

However, other things happened during this time. I kept thinking about Medjugorje and in April, 1992, I received a call from New York. A tour guide called to tell me that Father Jozo, the priest from St. James Church in Medjugorje, had just been making contacts at the United Nations, and he now says, "Anyone considering going to Medjugorje should go now, because the presence of U.S. citizens would be a protection for this small community which has, so far, never been harmed during the conflict."

The arrangements were made, and around June 20, a sizable group gathered in New York and took off for Medjugorje. Our first stop was Frankfort. I had no problems. I was in a wheel chair and was delivered everywhere. I was really given preferential treatment.

Our next stop was Zagreb, and then on to Split. At Split, we were placed on a bus for a four-hour trip along the Adriatic Sea. Since I was still given special privileges, the seat directly behind the bus driver was saved for me. We rode on winding roads, with what appeared to be very low 6 to 8 inch guard rails with several hundred foot drop-offs. I could not bear to look down.

About halfway on our bus trip, the bus stopped for a break of about twenty minutes. When it was time to leave, an old lady, dressed in black, a cigarette hanging from her mouth, jumped on, and very agilely went to the driver's area and took the seat in the very front, to the right of the driver. I didn't know anything about this since I could not speak their language, but she certainly noticed that I was afraid to look out the window, because I was hiding my eyes. She threw her sweater at me and motioned I could hide my eyes in it. She laughed at me, I thought, not with me. I had some feelings for her though, as she said, “You should not be afraid to die.” (She said this through our tour guide.)

Our tour guide told me, after speaking to this old lady for some time, “During the Second World War, the Germans came through and shot her husband. She remained on a small piece of land since that time, but now the Serbs have come through and have burned all the buildings. She left on foot and was now a refugee.” She is 85 years old and looks every day of it—this cigarette smoking, happy, full of life refugee, of whom I had become quite fond.

We finally arrived in Medjugorje. I remember it was over twenty-four hours since we began our journey. We arrived, but the luggage for the entire group was lost. No clothes, no shaving gear, nothing except what we were wearing. Some of the ladies carried a small bag, but I had nothing.

We were all provided with a great evening meal and then we retired. Again, I received preferential treatment. The owner’s wife tried to show me extra kindness—like two desserts. I needed that! The operators of this place, which was like a big house with several rooms built on and with a large dining room, were Marinko and Dragica Ivankovic.

Everything very simple—two people to a room, a mattress on a thin covered board on the floor, single size, and only one wood chair to share with my roommate. He had his own bed but that was it. We didn't know how to use the hot water system, so we only had cold water.

I had an idea and asked Dragica if she had a washing machine, and would she consider laundering my underwear and shirt. She made me feel very comfortable, and I know she was happy I asked. She even gave me some extras belonging to her husband. This was the beginning of a great relationship—more like a love-respect relationship.

Mornings, many went up Apparition Hill or the mountain, but I could do nothing but go to Marinko's porch, and so I visited with other pilgrims while drinking Marinko's European coffee. It was here I became a close acquaintance of a journalist from Galloway, Ireland. I could not get around and there was no way I could climb the hill, so I got to know Marinko and Dragica, even though our language was not compatible.

The English Mass at St. James was at 10:00 or 10:30 a.m.; the native Mass was at 6:00 p.m. They would sing the Litany of the Saints, beginning about 5:00 p.m. and also say the Rosary. I would take a cab back and forth, because there was no way I could walk.

One cab driver, with just a little English, told me all the cab drivers knew the limpy American—he pays 7 bucks. The cab fare was 2 bucks regardless of the number that would pile into the cab. I didn't think that 7 bucks was too much, because most of the time the car was filled with 5 to 6 passengers.

Shortly after we were in Medjugorje, the guide arranged meetings at the visionaries' homes. The first meeting was at Maria's home. She would speak to the people. I refused to go.

It was only about 50 feet away, so the guide questioned, "Why?" I told her I didn't come for that reason, and I was not chasing celebrities.

Another time I was invited to Vicka's, and again I refused. Then I was invited to the tower to be present at an apparition. Again, I refused, even though the numbers would have been limited and I should have felt privileged. The truth was, I was intent on spending all my time in the Church before the Blessed Sacrament. That was true until June 25.

That morning the guide came to me and said, "Listen, before you refuse again, Dragica feels so sorry for you because you cannot walk, and she wants to take only you to Ivanka's house for her apparition, which she only has on June 25 each year. Marinko and Dragica will take you." I could not refuse.

That evening, Marinko took me, along with Dragica, in his auto to Ivanka's house. It was about 15 minutes away and when we arrived, I noticed many automobiles around the house. This didn't stop Dragica. Marinko drove on Ivanka's lawn and parked very close to her house. Dragica got out of the car and pulled me out by the hand, and continued pulling me into the house and through a huge crowd of people, and stopped directly in back of Ivanka's station before the Crucifix, which was now occupied by Jelena, who many people are familiar with.

She was leading the Rosary...only I thought this was Ivanka. Then the time for the arrival of the Gospa came, and Ivanka entered the room and replaced Jelena. I knew when Our Lady appeared because Ivanka went from a standing position to her knees so hard, that the bang on the floor made a loud noise. I thought Ivanka's knee caps should be broken. I had read about how the children did this at Garabandal.

I was so overwhelmed during the apparition, I could not take my eyes off Ivanka and where she seemed to be staring. I saw every stripe in her dress, dark blue and white; every seam; and every curl in her hair. All the time I kept repeating silently, "Holy Mary, Mother of God!" ...an exclamation. "Holy Mary, Mother of God?" ...a question. "Right here in front of me? Holy Mary, Mother of God," ...in awe.

I think I repeated this 50 times during the 15 minutes of the apparition. Then Ivanka raised both her hands as though reaching. I could understand nothing anyway, so I asked nothing. No big deal! Then Ivanka put her hands down and turned around, crying profusely. Dragica took both her own hands and put them on the forearm of Ivanka and forced her to shake my hand.

"Nice," I thought, but after it was explained, through an English interpreter, what the message was and that, at the end, Ivanka raised her hands to hold the hands of the Blessed Mother, then it was hard to believe that she shook my hand. This night was extremely emotional. It was a brush with the supernatural, and I kept repeating, "Holy Mary, Mother of God."

Marinko then drove me to St. James Church. We couldn't even get on the church grounds; there were so many people. We were in the street. I didn't care. I was with Holy Mary, Mother of God in my mind then. I didn't come close to sleeping all night, and I was still awake when the famous Medjugorje rooster started crowing.

June 26...I am still on a high. I took a cab to go to the 10:00 a.m. English Mass. There were others in the cab with me, and when we arrived at the Church, as close as the cab could get us, the others got out and were standing in a semi-circle around the door which I was exiting.

I had my hand wrapped around the door post and Sheila slammed the door shut with great force. Another one of our group saw my hand and tried to catch the door but missed. The door reached my four fingers, stopped and gently opened again all the way. I pulled my hand back, clenched my fist, and placed it behind my back. I was afraid to look. The cab driver was yelling for ice water. I was thinking, "Four smashed fingers (if they are still there), no hospital, no doctors, no way out for four days, and I can barely walk."

Then I thought, "When is it going to start to hurt?" I slowly brought my hand to the front of me and I could see slight creases on my fingers which disappeared while I was looking at them. I glanced toward the heavens and, with a slight chuckle, said, "OK, I owe You one." This last 24 hours was very special, and the day continued with everything going through my mind over and over again.

That evening, I went to the Croatian Mass which was very crowded. At the Sign of Peace, I looked down the pew and I spotted the 85-year-old lady from the bus. She spotted me at the same time and we both made an effort to reach each other. The four people between us were moved like bowling pins. I was so happy to see her. Later, I learned that she was taken in by Marinko and Dragica, who fed and housed her, along with about 6 or 7 other refugees. I was very impressed by the charity of Marinko and Dragica.

The next day I asked our guide to interpret so I could speak to Marinko and Dragica. I asked them if I could help in any way to support the 85-year-old lady. After all, Marinko and Dragica could not take care of the whole nation. Marinko said, “How would you do that?” I said, “I'll give you a check.” He said, “I can cash the check, but the government will take half of it. Communists, you know.” I told him I didn't have any cash dollars with me.

Here is where the journalist from Gallaway, Ireland rescued us. He suggested, “Send me the check. I will cash it and mount it in a picture frame. I will then send it with some pilgrims going to Medjugorje, and they will give the picture to Marinko. He will take the back off and there will be the cash. No problem.”

We continued to do this for several months. The journalist's name, by the way, is Sean Connery. Leaving these kind people to return home was very difficult, Marinko and Dragica especially.

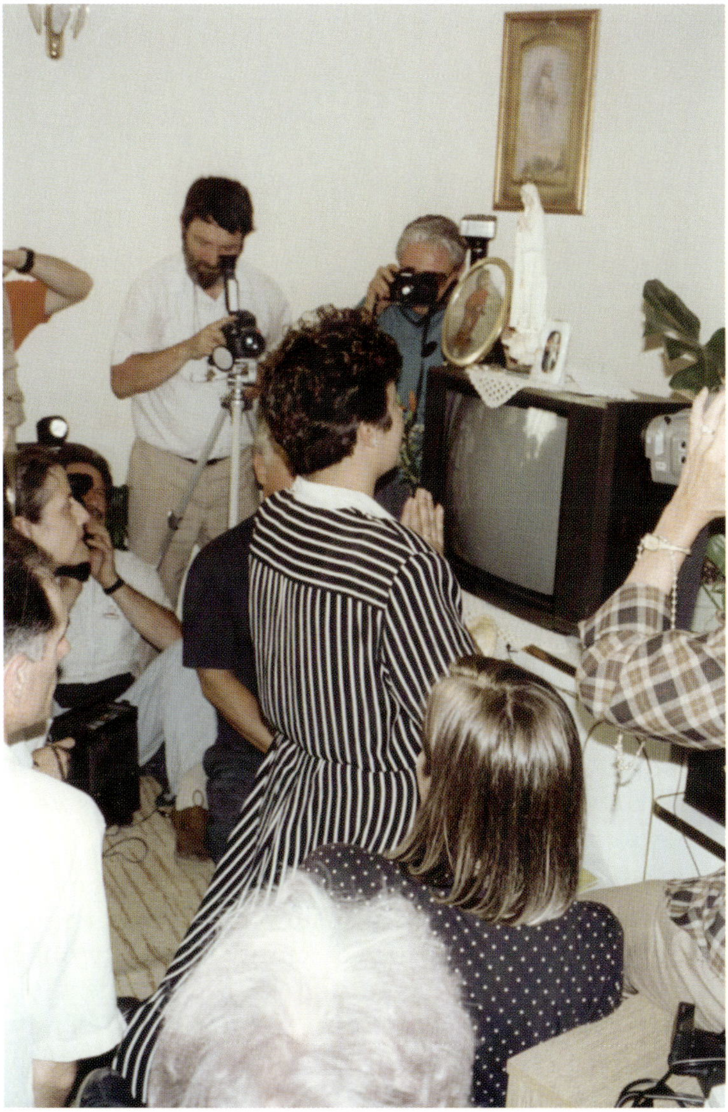

Above: My first presence at an apparition, Ivanka's home in Medjugorje

Chapter 4

Visits With Ivan

A few months later, I received a very strange phone call. It went something like this: "I want to ask you a question, but I do not want an answer at this time." I said, "What is it?" This person said, "No...first I need your promise that you will not divulge the content to anyone." I said, "OK. I will only tell one person." I even told them who this person was. However, I received a rapid fire answer, "No, you can't." I said, "OK, OK."

"You must pray about this for 6 weeks," they said. I said, "I don't know how to do that." They said, "We want to know if you would consider becoming involved in a project with Ivan Dragicevic?" I asked, "What is it?" They told me they would call back in 6 weeks and they would tell me then.

This was most difficult to me. I had no clue as to what this was. I couldn't tell anyone. I didn't even know if I should be sad, glad, scared, or whatever. I wondered a lot about it and 6 weeks went by—not a word. Then 8 weeks. I totally relaxed. I thought, "Whatever this is, I think it passed over and I can forget about it."

Well, one day I received another phone call, and was asked "What is your answer?" I replied, "How can I refuse? How can I refuse becoming involved with someone who sees and speaks to Our Lady everyday? Certainly!" I said.

Then they said, "Then Ivan wants to meet you. He wants to visit you." I thought, "Oh, no-o-o-o." I'm not good at this, so I said, "Oh, that will not be necessary at all." They asked, "Do you mean you do not want to meet Ivan?" I told them, "No. I just don't think it is necessary." They replied, "He will visit you."

The truth was, I wondered where he would visit me. Is he going to come by my office? Does he want to meet somewhere else, or at my home? I had no idea and I was afraid to ask. I was very scared. At that time, I was a single 64-year-old man, living with a brother 78 years old, and in no position to bring someone like this into my house. How can I entertain or have a person of this stature for a meal?

I was told it would be in several weeks and I was glad. I felt, the longer the better, and maybe they'll forget. I told a lady about this and she was happy about it.

Several months later, a phone call came. They informed me they would be here in about 3 weeks. Then, they said, "Where can we stay?" I replied, "Well, I have two furnished, empty bedrooms upstairs." They said, "Good, we will stay with you." I asked, "Who, and for how long?" They said, "Ivan, and he will bring an interpreter. They will stay one night only." I reluctantly said, "OK."

I then told the happy lady about my misfortune, and she suggested, "Another lady and I will come to your house, cook the meals, get all the supplies, arrange to have 10 for meals and 30 to 35 for an apparition and you don't have to do a thing." I thought, "Can all this be really happening?" Yes it did, but even more. It was an experience so awesome, that words cannot really describe the emotional experience.

Ivan has remained in touch ever since, like every 10 to 15 days, many times oftener, and just about from anywhere in the world. He has been to my home often, always overnight, and usually about 2 to 3 days at a time. Someone asked me, one time, "Does it get less meaningful after a number of times?" I remember the lady who asked, and I replied, "Just the opposite."

Our project lasted a few years, and I have never divulged the content of the first question. I don't think I could divulge it if I tried.

I believe my relationship with Ivan was planned and arranged by Our Lady. I believe She is the reason and the cause. I will do all She asks. She will not ask what I am not able to carry out, but She knows how I feel. She is my best friend. I talk to Her all the time.

I asked a friend, one time, "Do you ever pray to Our Lady?" He said, "Oh, yes." I said, "Where is She when you pray to Her? Is She in Heaven?"

"Certainly," he replied. I asked, "Do you look to the heavens for help?"

"Sure," he said. "Don't you?"

I told him that I believe Our Lady is always by my side. I talk to Her and She takes care of me. There are times I believe She wants me to know what She is going to do before She does it. I told him that I would give him some examples later.

I always share my every experience with Brother Stephen. I asked him, "Sometime, when Ivan comes, could you come to an apparition?" He replied, "I doubt that it would ever be possible."

Statue of Our Lady in the Apparition Room in Dubuque

Chapter 5

My Friend Is Very Ill

On Monday, Jan. 8, 1993, at 2:15 p.m., I received a phone call from Dragica from Medjugorje. "Please, George, pray. Marinko, my husband, is in hospital, very sick. We are in Zagreb with son. Here is phone number—0113841229079. Talk to daughter now. "I asked the daughter what was wrong, and she answered, "Don't know yet." I thought she also said, "Something inside. He very sick." But I couldn't be sure. Language is a problem.

This phone call just about blew me away. I thought, "Your front door is approximately 50' away from Maria's front door, directly across the street. You live about 4 doors away from Vicka and one block from Ivan and Marianna. Why didn't you call them? (Or maybe they did, I don't know.) How is it you call Dubuque, Iowa?" I was just awestruck.

After I hung up, I called a lady in Wichita, Kansas...she speaks the language...she also received a call from Zagreb. It seems that Marinko has tumors on the colon and on the liver. She had concerns that he would be unable to get proper care there and should be taken elsewhere. The war was going on in Yugoslavia and the hospitals were so overcrowded, there were some beds with two patients. But, Dragica and Marinko cannot think about going elsewhere because they have no insurance good for anyplace else, and so cannot afford to go anywhere else.

When I finished speaking with this lady, I called a doctor friend, Dr. Denis Faber, and I explained the situation to him, and then asked, "If I could get him out of his country to Mayo Clinic, would you have any connections there?" He said to me, "If his life can be extended with quality care and without a long extended after-treatment, bring him to Dubuque."

He went on to say, "It sounds like cancer which has traveled through the blood stream. It is not a good sign. You know that I will do everything that I can. I can turn you to the proper people and in the proper direction, but we need first, to get some medical records to study." I felt this was not an easy task from here, but was determined to try.

I called the lady in Wichita back, and told her the entire conversation. She said, "May I tell Dragica?" and I said, "Yes." Then she said, "Let's go to Zagreb, you and I." A little surprised, I told her I would let her know in the morning. I immediately placed a call to a convent of good Sisters and asked for prayers. I was told, "We will give it our Industrial Strength prayers."

At 6 p.m., I received a call from the Mother Superior. She said, "Sweetheart, why are you sad?" I explained, and our conversation lasted a long time. I told her about the call to my doctor friend, and then asked her, "Mother, what should I do?" She answered, "George, you must do what the Spirit tells you."

I remember the time of day, the tone of her voice, and the compassion in her heart. She really put me at ease, and then I had to leave for my chapel time. I said, "Hey Mary, You need to talk to Your Son about Marinko. He will only die if Your Son allows it. I think Marinko is too important to allow that at this time."

Mary and I talked about this for the next hour. Actually, I did all the talking, but I was never in doubt about Her carrying out my request. She always answered me, but I also know that She has a lot to do with what I ask.

The next day I called the lady in Wichita, and asked, "When do we leave for Zagreb?" She told me that she had talked to Marinko's son, and was told that Marinko was to undergo further tests and we should get those results first before we leave. It was decided that we would go the next week and I was satisfied with that.

Later that same evening, I received another call from the Mother Superior. "How is your friend?" I told her I thought I would go to Zagreb, and she said, "I think that would be very nice of you. I will pray for your safety. When do you leave?"

I told her it would probably be the next week, and she explained that she would be leaving for Europe on Friday, Feb. 12, and would be back on the 21. We would speak then. We talked for a good while after this, and I felt much better.

A couple of days later, again I tried calling Zagreb. I couldn't get through to them, but kept trying all day. Impossible! The next day I called Wichita at 8:00 a.m. My friend said, “I was just looking up your number to call you. Marinko is healed! I think it must be a miracle. What else could it be? He was x-rayed in Chitluk and diagnosed. Then again in Zagreb and the diagnosis was the same. Spots on the colon and liver. Now he is well. They can no longer find anything. Please call him. He wants to talk to you. I just talked to him.”

I called and finally made connections at 4:00 p.m. I talked to Marinko and all he could say was, “George, oh, George. My friend! My friend! Thank you, thank you, thank you.” I didn't know what he was talking about, but he was full of joy. I asked, “How do you feel?” He said, “Much better. Much better. Much, much better.” Language was again a big problem.

Dragica got on the phone and expressed great joy and gratitude, and then the daughter also had to speak to me. I explained I had mailed a letter two weeks previously, along with some pictures, to two addresses—one in Zagreb and one in Medjugorje. I asked them to watch for the letter. They had asked for copies of the pictures that I took while there.

That is about it. What happened? I truly don't know. I feel that if you want to know more, you need to go to a higher being. But, I was not surprised then, nor am I now, as I recall it. I was not expecting a miracle but, at all times, felt what happened could very well happen. I could not pray for him to get well. Only, "Hey, Mary, hold him, embrace him and console Dragica and the family."

I knew, when I spoke to Our Lady and Our Lord, They were before me in the Blessed Sacrament and They were also in Marinko's presence. At one time, I said, "Hey Mary, say Hi to Marinko for me." I was always aware of our link—Our Lady!

This is not the end of the story, however. I didn't know what to say to my doctor friend. One day I tell him that my friend is in bad shape and needs help. Now, 10 days later, I should tell him that my friend is in good shape and nothing is wrong? As a result, I did not say anything until about a month later. I was in the Post Office and saw the doctor at a considerable distance away. He sees me, too, and calls, quite loudly, "Hey, George, what happened to our friend?" I yelled back, "He's been healed." The doctor said, "Oh. Went to a higher power, eh?"...embarrassed, I said, "Yeah." Embarrassed because I had not gotten back to him and kept him informed.

Six months later, Ivan Dragicevic, visionary from Medjugorje whose home is approximately one block from Marinko's, is coming to Dubuque and will have an apparition at my house, and the lady from Witchita will interpret for him. I really wanted to make it up to the doctor, so I invited him and his wife. They consented to come. Now they can meet the "in-between" person between Marinko and us.

Before the apparition started, and finding out the Rosary was going to be said, my doctor friend asked me if anyone had an extra Rosary with him, as he didn't bring one. This is never a problem, as someone is sure to bring extras.

One of the ladies there had an extra Rosary in her purse. It was a memento of her husband who had died about 6 months previously. He had been in an institution for a number of years at Independence. She let it be known that she would allow the doctor to use it, but that she wanted it back.

A couple of minutes later, the doctor's wife tapped me on the shoulder and, in shock and awe, said, "George, look, this is my husband's Rosary. His name is inscribed on the back of the crucifix. I gave it to him 25 years ago for our anniversary, and then he lost it. He didn't know where it was." I thought, "Oh, my!"

It was time for the Rosary, and then Ivan came in for the apparition. Afterwards, there was a great deal of emotion and excitement, as bit by bit the story of the Rosary unfolded. I am certain that, in the lady's purse she had her husband's Rosary, but now, in the doctor's hand, it became his Rosary. (Sure reminds me of the bread and wine.)

About 4 days later, the doctor's wife called to find out the lady's name who gave them the Rosary. It was an awesome mystery that evening, and it is an awesome mystery to this day, years later. If anyone involved felt any skepticism, this should have blown it away.

Chapter 6

Pilgrimage To Medjugorje

September 28, 1994, an apparition was planned, and I asked Brother Stephen to participate. I told him, "You must ask." He got back to me and said that the request was denied. This was about ten days before the 28th.

On the morning of the 28th, Brother Stephen called about 8:00 o'clock. He said, "Is that invitation still open for me to be present with Ivan?"

"Why, yes, of course," I replied. He told me that the Abbot had changed his mind and would allow him to come. This made everything better for me, for Brother Stephen, for Ivan, and for Our Lady, I think.

It was at that time that Ivan had asked me to come to Medjugorje again. I didn't say "yes or no." Later, I asked Ivan if it was possible for me to invite Brother Stephen and a Sister Marie Louise to join me, and Ivan said, "No problem." This is one of Ivan's favorite expressions.

I asked Brother Stephen, and this time he said, "I don't think we have a chance. It has never happened that a member of any Trappist community in the United States has ever been allowed to leave the nation except the Abbot." But, he said he would ask. I reminded him that if Our Lady wants him there, he will be there. What an unbelievable reply from the Abbot—"Permission granted."

The following is a description of our trip to Medjugorje in July 1995, written by Brother Stephen: *Pilgrimage to Medjugorje in Bosnia-Herzegovina...*

So many have asked me about my pilgrimage to Medjugorje, wanting to know why I went there, and what my impressions are of the visionaries and their story, and whether or not it was dangerous to be there because of the war, that I decided to write an account of this trip.

In the Fall of 1994, George Banworth, a person whom I have known since the mid-1960's, invited me to go with him and another guest to Medjugorje, a small village in former Yugoslavia, where six children began seeing the Blessed Virgin Mary on June 24, 1981.

The Abbot knew this was an unusual offer, but he remembered that two monks from our Trappist community in England had already made a pilgrimage there, and so there was a precedent for approving it. He told me I could accept the invitation, and after various delays, the trip was finally arranged for the first two weeks of this month.

We flew from Chicago to Prague on Czechoslovakian Airlines, and then from Prague to

Split, which is the second largest city in former Yugoslavia, situated midway on the western coastline along the Adriatic Sea. From there we traveled by van in-land to Medjugorje, crossing the beautiful mountains and valleys that make up the landscape of Bosnia.

The closest well known city to Medjugorje is Mostar, which suffered from repeated shelling by the Bosnian Serbs in the earlier stages of the war. Sarajevo is less than 100 miles away, but several hours by car because of the twisting mountain roads. The war is too far away to affect the cities near Medjugorje at present. However, we saw many convoys of U.N. trucks moving along the roads from Split to Sarajevo bringing supplies to help the people survive.

The conflict is between the Serbs, who are Greek Orthodox, and the Croats, who are Roman Catholic, with the Muslims caught in the middle. The Serbs are twice as populous with 10 1/2 million people compared to the approximate 5 million Croats. Being more numerous, the Serbs have settled outside their homeland of Serbia over the years, mainly in Bosnia-Herzegovina which borders the west side of Serbia.

They now comprise 31% of Bosnia's population while controlling 65% of the land. The Muslims comprise 44% of the population but only possess 5% of the land. The Croats make up the difference, and they also control the area called Croatia, which is predominately north and northwest of Bosnia. Although they speak the same language, Serbs use the Cyrillic alphabet like the Russians, while Croats use the Roman alphabet. During the Second World

War, Hitler's forces over-ran Croatia, but were fought off by the Serbs. In postwar Yugoslavia, the Croats had to accept a satellite status under domination by Tito's partisans, many of whom were Serbs.

After the death of Tito in 1980, and the collapse of the Soviet empire about 9 years later, the Serbs began land-grabbing to bring the Bosnian Serbs into an independent Greater Serbia, while using a process of ethnic cleansing to kill or displace the Muslims and Croats in the more northeastern areas of Bosnia-Herzegovina.

The extremely rugged terrain, mountainous with heavy vegetation, makes it ideal for guerrilla warfare. The cities are more vulnerable. So, the Serbs have been attacking the cities and trying to destroy the people as they flee. The war is so cruel, and human solutions are so fragile that it may be that Heaven has opened and Mary has appeared to ask, over and over, for peace and reconciliation, for a return to faith, prayer, conversion, and penance, in order to replace hatred with love.

The people living in Medjugorje have always been deeply religious, compared to the majority of cities around the world. In 1933, they decided to commemorate the nineteenth hundred anniversary of Christ's death on the Cross by putting up a 45-foot tall concrete cross on top of the nearest mountain, which rises some 1,500 feet above the valley.

The climb is extremely rugged, with jagged stones all the way. The peasant women carried up water and the peasant men carried up the concrete. Today this huge concrete cross dominates the view of several surrounding valleys.

The mountain was renamed Mt. Krizevac, i.e. the Mountain of the Cross.

The path to the top of the mountain now is lined by the 14 Stations of the Cross, and it is a favorite place for pilgrims who come to pray and do penance. It took me 40 minutes to climb it one evening, after the heat of the day had passed. I felt a little apprehensive about how well my jogging shoes would hold up against the sharp jagged rocks, boulders, and stones.

Then, on my way down, I was put to shame by some other pilgrims, middle-aged women from Ireland, who were climbing the mountain in their bare feet! Every Friday there is a group of the local peasants with one of the Franciscan priests who climb the mountain making the Stations of the Cross as they go, and many pilgrims join them.

The people of Medjugorje are remarkable for another sign of their deep faith. In 1937, they decided to build a new church. Construction was interrupted by the war and then continued during the postwar years, and completed in 1969. This is a small village area, too small for the large church they built, capable of holding about 1,700 people. But, today this same church is actually too small for the crowds of pilgrims who come there.

Outside the church, in a large patio, there are rows upon rows of park benches to accommodate the overflow of people. The liturgy is broadcast to the people outside by loudspeakers so that they can follow the Mass, and Holy Communion is distributed outside, because the aisles inside are usually crowded with people who could not find room in the pews.

Yet another sign of the strong faith of the people occurred right after the end of World War II. When the Communists took over Yugoslavia, they came upon a Franciscan monastery at Siroki Brijeg, about 45 minutes from Medjugorje where 30 friars lived. They were told to take off their habits and to trample upon the crucifix of Christ or else be shot.

Not one of them would do it. So all of them were martyred, first by being shot and then burned to death. The mother of one of the martyrs was so overcome with grief and tears for the loss of her priest-son, that her youngest boy, just a lad, tried to console her by saying that he would become a priest and take his older brother's place as a Franciscan.

That boy, I was told, is Fr. Jozo Zovko, who became the parish priest at the church in Medjugorje a few months before the apparitions of Mary began in 1981. He, himself, did not at first believe the story of the six children when they came to him for protection from the police, until Our Lady gave him a sign of the reality of Her appearances.

The Communists tried to suppress the outburst of devotion that followed the beginning of the visions. They arrested Fr. Jozo and submitted him to torture. It took a full year and a half before the Franciscans were able to gain his release, and then it was under condition that he would not be reassigned to Medjugorje.

So, today he is stationed at the same place where the 30 Franciscans were martyred. Since he cannot meet the pilgrims who come to Medjugorje, they now go to meet him at his church, and listen to his story about the first appearances of Our Lady and the meaning of Her messages. He has been known to talk to the pilgrims for hours, but during my trip, he spoke to our group for just an hour and then celebrated Mass for us.

Most of the pilgrims are married people with families. His most urgent message was the need for families to pray together in their homes with their children. Who else will teach children to pray if their parents do not pray with them? Above all else, he said that each home should have a special place where a Crucifix, a statue or icon of Mary, a Bible, and a Rosary should be kept. Few homes lack television sets, but how many lack a place for prayers!

When I reflect on the faith of these people from Medjugorje, it is not so surprising to me that Mary would appear among them. What is amazing is that Our Lady urged them to conversion! She asked them to increase their faith, to deepen their prayer life, to fast more often, to seek reconciliation and peace with others. If these people needed a message like that, where do we stand?

Even their manner of greeting one another is a prayer. They say, "Praise be Jesus and Mary," and the one being greeted responds, "Jesus and Mary, forever." I learned to say these words in Croatian so I could share their greetings, and my heart was lifted up by it every time.

A year after the apparitions began, Our Lady asked them to start prayer groups. Ivan, who was then 17, began a group that has met together twice a week for several hours for the past thirteen years. Sometimes they meet on the site where the apparitions first began, a mountainous hillside at the edge of the village, up a steep and rugged path that is now lined by large copper icons commemorating the Mysteries of the Rosary.

Pilgrims always want to climb this hillside, to the spot where Mary appeared, and pray there. It is marked by a simple iron cross about ten feet tall, under which the stones are becoming worn and rounded by the shoes and bare feet of so many people. Sometimes people from Medjugorje, along with the pilgrims, climb the hillside at night carrying candles or flashlights, praying the Rosary out loud, and singing hymns that can be heard in the streets and houses below.

One of the members of Ivan's prayer group is now 30 years old. He helps manage a place for recovering drug addicts called Campo della Vita (Camp of Life.) It was founded by an Italian nun named Sister Elvira who has established 17 similar places around the world. The one in Medjugorje is located about a block from the home of Ivan and Laureen, where we stayed for the two weeks we were there, so it was a short walk away.

About 50 to 65 drug addicts live at the Camp, following a life style that is monastic. They are building the living quarters and workshops themselves from the native stones. They have no TV, no radio, no newspapers, no smoking, no alcohol, no girls, and of course...no drugs.

Several times a day they come together for prayer. They do not leave except in the company of other members. The youngest is 15 and the oldest is 42. They stay as long as needed to fully overcome their addiction. It may take a couple years, or ten years.

As one of the members gave us a tour, I saw men digging out deep basement foundations for new buildings, cracking large boulders with sledge hammers; others were working in an icon studio creating some of the most beautiful religious art I have ever seen. Others were working in the farm area with the livestock—cows, chickens, pigs, etc.

Their chapel is the work of their own labor, and its beauty captures one's heart as quickly as the beauty of New Melleray's Church. Since it was the middle of the afternoon, they were all at work, and I did not see them gathered for prayer. But I was told their singing is so beautiful that CD recordings were made, and income from the sale of these CD's helps support them.

One of the six children who first saw Our Lady is named Vicka. Today she is 31 years old, and she is the most outgoing and friendly of the six. She does the cooking and some of the sewing for these drug addicts. The example of her humble service of these men makes me admire her all the more, and adds more certainty to her credibility and her testimony about the appearances of the Blessed Virgin Mary.

At that time, Vicka was not married. She was the only one of the six who still lived year-round at Medjugorje. I asked if there has been a foundation of one of Sister Elvira's 17 houses in the United States, and learned that she has one in St. Augustine, Florida.

The village of Medjugorje today combines an old country atmosphere with new world commercialism. Tourist shops have sprung up to meet the demands of the pilgrims for religious articles. Four-story hotels with modern conveniences are being erected next to small one-room dwellings that have existed for decades or even centuries.

The narrow rough roads made for wagons and carts are now crowded with small European cars whose drivers dash about in apparent unconcern for the life and property of others. It was much safer to walk along narrow paths through the fields than to follow the roads.

Along the path through the fields, which was about a mile long, an elderly woman displayed her crocheting in hopes that passing pilgrims would buy some of her handiwork. Here the old country flavor still prevails along the rows of vineyards and wheat fields. A woman might be leading a cow along by a chain to a small pasture; a middle-aged couple and their son and daughter could be seen putting up hay with pitchforks into a large stack; a young boy nearby was playing with two doves he had tamed; and a smaller boy was frolicking naked in a large tub of water.

By contrast, at the end of the country path, there was a small hotel with a large chartered bus parked on one side, and several cars with the sign "Taxi" mounted on top of them. One of the favorite English words adopted by the local people is posted in front of many shops in their own peculiar spelling: "DISKONT."

Almost all of the clerks in stores know enough English to assist the English-speaking pilgrims. Soft drinks, ice cream, hamburgers, pizza, and other familiar foods are readily available. The Croatian cuisine is much like that of the Italians, which I love. I was afraid they would have fish most of the time (which I don't love) and that I would end up losing weight. Instead, I relished their food and gained several pounds.

One afternoon, we went to visit Marinko Ivankovic and his lovely wife. They treated us to a four-course dinner that satisfied my hunger for several days. He is a middle-aged man who knew the six children from the time they were born. In several cases, he was even an alter-parent for them because of the frequent absences of their own parents who had to travel out of the country for work.

This compassionate and loving man, who is so easy to approach, was one of the first persons the children told of the vision they had seen when Mary first appeared. As we sat at his table he told us the story of those early days in the middle of 1981. Having known the children for so long, he was immediately certain they were not lying. And, he went to the priests to urge them to speak with and examine the children.

When the Communist police began trying to suppress what was happening, they took Marinko to jail. He did not know what they were going to do to him. Since they did not believe in the possibility of supernatural visions, they suspected he might have been the cause of the children's claims, but they were puzzled why he hadn't put his own children up to the claim of seeing Mary, rather than someone else's children.

He simply told them, "Because my children did not see Her, and these others did!" Marinko was beaten and finally released. Meanwhile, his wife was nearly out of her mind with fear for his safety. As we listened to their memories of those days, I was struck by their sheer goodness and sincerity, and by the enormity of the privilege they had received in being close to these events.

This first-person account left me with no doubt of the truth that Mary appeared to these children. As we were leaving the warmth of their home and their hospitality following such a wonderful meal, I heard Marinko's wife saying, "Oh, my God, I forgot the ice cream." They invited us for a meal again the next week, and this time she remembered the ice cream!

Four of the six children continue to see Mary every day, even after 16 years! Many pilgrims have witnessed miraculous events such as the dance of the sun in the sky, or Rosaries turning to gold, or physical healings. Greater still are the conversions of so many people from mediocrity to fervent generosity and love.

One exceptional physical healing, through the intercession of Mary's appearances in Medjugorje, is the case of an American woman born in Dubuque. She had been crippled and deformed by MS for 26 years, when all of a sudden, she was healed in a single day. Her name is Rita Klaus, and she has written a book about her experience, titled "Rita's Story."

The healing took place in 1986, and she has visited Medjugorje frequently in gratitude ever since. By a happy coincidence, she was there when I was, and stayed at the house of Ivan's brother across the road. We talked several times together. I am now reading her book and find it very interesting. I feel that I have met a friend.

Even though the visions are still taking place, they are kept very private, so that pilgrims are focused not on the apparitions as such, but on the meaning and purpose of Our Lady's appearances; the call to conversion and return to the Sacraments and the life of prayer, voluntary self-denial, reconciliation with others, and peace with love.

Mr. Banworth, Sr. Marie Louise Murphy, and I were staying with Ivan and Laureen in their beautiful home for the two weeks we were in Medjugorje. We were allowed to be present each day when Mary appeared to Ivan as we prayed the Rosary together. These apparitions took place in the small building called the Adoration Chapel, which is near the large Church of St. James. The Blessed Sacrament is exposed for adoration all day long, so that the pilgrims can come and pray there at anytime.

Most of my afternoons were passed in this chapel, as I prayed a decade of the Rosary for each of my friends and relatives by name in turn. It was a wonderful experience of having so much time to linger and intercede for all those whom I love. Mr. B and Sister Marie Louise were doing the same thing, and around the middle of the afternoon, we would go for a treat of lemonade and ice cream.

Many people passed through that chapel from different countries, all of them stopping to pray and adore, to love and intercede...just as we were doing. I felt a great sense of unity with each of them and encouragement from their example of faith and devotion.

Towards evening, at the time of day when Mary appears to the four visionaries wherever they may be, Ivan came to the Adoration Chapel. A few people, like ourselves, were allowed to stay.

We prayed the Rosary until Her appearance to him. Then we knelt in silence while he saw the vision. We could see nothing except his responses (all in silence) to the presence that was beyond our senses. Afterwards, when Our Lady had left, he ended with some vocal prayers out loud in his own language.

There was nothing supernatural evident to anyone else that would confirm he was actually seeing Our Lady. If we had to rely on what we could see and hear, it would not be possible to declare he was actually seeing Her. Belief in the ongoing appearances of Mary to Ivan or the other visionaries, depends on their own testimony that it is still happening.

But, that is a credible testimony because of the things that have happened in the past 14 years, and because it is bearing such good fruit among the people who come there. I find it easier to believe She continues to appear to them, than that they would be able to live a continuing lie every day about such things that affect their own souls and the souls of so many others.

Perhaps one of them could carry out such a lie over a long time because of some mental sickness, but not all of them together. Many professional medical and psychiatric examinations have already been performed to discern whether they are lying or telling truthfully what they have been experiencing. There has been no evidence destroying their story.

Yet, in some ways, I was disappointed that the apparitions of Our Lady every day did not have a more apparent visible affect on the visionaries. I would like to have seen a glow on Ivan's face after he finished seeing Mary each day, and an unruffled sense of peace, or a bubbling over with joy. Instead, he was little different from any of us after we finished praying the Rosary.

But then, I can ask myself, how different am I after I receive that greatest of miracles each day, the Eucharist, the Body and Blood of Jesus Christ! I realized that the visionaries carry a heavy burden, the weight of their own weaknesses and sins. Like all of us, and maybe more, they, too, need prayers.

Ivan has dedicated his life to the youth of the world, going out to them to teach them about Christ and Mary and all the wonders of our faith. At the time of this writing, he is in England giving a conference called Youth 2000 at Ampleforth Abbey. Young people come from all over to hear him. At the end of August he will travel throughout the United States until March of 1996, to bring Our Lady's messages to all who will listen. Then he will go to Australia and Rome before returning to Medjugorje next Spring.

Yet, he is human and would probably prefer more relaxing things like watching basketball, which he absolutely loves, or playing soccer as he does each Sunday afternoon. He is good at it, so good that his face was on the front cover of Sport Magazine as player of the year. Ironically, the same issue had a note in the upper left-hand corner saying: "Swim Suit Issue." He also likes to drive like crazy. When he took us to see Fr. Jozo, I noticed the highway sign said 40 kmh, and he was going 90!

There is one experience which I found more meaningful than anything else at Medjugorje. It was the experience of catholicity, which comes from a Greek word meaning "completely whole" or all inclusive or universal. I saw people from many different nations coming with the same love, faith, and devotion that I had. Only our languages and customs were different.

They came from France, England, Ireland, Canada, United States, Australia, Italy, New Zealand, Uganda, Czechoslovakia, Poland, etc. But, all of us came together with the same beliefs and the same love of the Sacraments. Being among all these people made me realize in a new way how great is the faith I share with them.

It unites all of us in a common belief of where we came from, where we are going, and the way to live as we prepare for our eternal future. And, we expressed it together when we gathered in the Adoration Chapel before the Blessed Sacrament, or as we came together for the evening liturgy at 7:00 p.m. in the Church of St. James. Although we could not understand the local language of the people, we sat with them and with each other, celebrating the liturgy which belongs to all peoples of all times. The devotions of the local people actually begin at 6:00 p.m. with public Rosaries and hymns. At 7:00 the Mass begins.

For the Gospel, each concelebrating priest representing a different language group reads the Gospel of the day in his own language. This often means as many as a half dozen repetitions of the day's Gospel. The prayers of consecration are said in Latin for the convenience of the visiting priests of different nationalities. The Mass ends around ten minutes after eight, and then there are more devotions until 9:00 p.m. And, they do this every night!

A week before we arrived, there were 60,000 pilgrims at Medjugorje because of the 14th anniversary of Mary's first appearance there in 1981. During the two weeks we were there, only 300 to 500 pilgrims came. But, coming from so many places and expressing the same faith made me realize how much I love them all, not just those I live with every day, but people all over the world.

During the day, the pilgrims also have the opportunity to celebrate a Mass in their own language. The English Mass is always at 10:00 a.m. One day, I wanted to watch how the other pilgrims celebrated their liturgies. So, I stayed for a Mass in French, and in German, and in Czech, and of course Croatian.

Of them all, I was most impressed by the French. Their singing and their reverence left me spellbound. And, there were so many young people among them. In fact, everywhere I looked, young adults and teenagers of every nationality were sharing the enthusiasm of the middle-aged and the elderly.

One exception. I passed an American couple one afternoon near the chapel. They had a boy about eight years old who was repeating in a pleading tone, "No more church, no more church!" And he was right...he needed time to play.

The story of Medjugorje involves much more than I can ever tell. Here, at New Melleray, we have 35 books that have a few chapters or are entirely about Medjugorje. There is a new movie being shown in theaters around the country today about the events involving Fr. Jozo at Medjugorje, called "Gospa." Martin Sheen plays the leading role.

Ivan's lovely wife, Laureen, an Irish American from Boston, grew up without having a deep understanding or love of the Catholic faith. She won the beauty pageant for Massachusetts in 1989. Then she and a friend and two cousins went to Medjugorje out of curiosity. Her two cousins were ordinary fun-loving kids without any real interest in religion. But, their experience transformed all their lives. She fell in love with Ivan and discovered the richness of her faith at the same time.

Her two cousins returned to America and entered the seminary to become priests. Laureen was now expecting her first child on October 4. Since the hospitals are still very inadequate in Bosnia, she will be in Boston to have her baby, and Ivan will be with her. I feel very grateful to them for letting me share in their lives and their hope. I am also so grateful to Mr. B. for inviting me to go with him and Sr. Marie Louise. It was wonderful! Praise be Jesus and Mary! (End of Brother Stephen's description of the trip.)

Brother Stephen truly enjoyed the trip, and I just want to say, "No one could ever have such a great trip with such a great Brother and a great Sister. No, not ever. It cannot be any better." And, I also realized at this time that a strong friendship had been established between Ivan and Brother Stephen.

Only recently I have learned why Brother Stephen became very preoccupied one day while in Medjugorje. Following is his explanation of what happened:

"About forty years ago, my brother could no longer participate in the Sacraments because he remarried several years after being divorced. I was already a monk of New Melleray Abbey at the time. Knowing the power of prayer, I interceded for him every day. Years went by...nothing happened. After twenty-five years, I began complaining to God, "This is taking an awfully long time!" In my heart, I heard the Lord respond, "What are you doing about it?"

"Me! What am I supposed to do?" I thought about it, and the next time I spoke to my brother on the phone, I asked him, "Have you ever thought about finding out if your first marriage was invalid?" He wasn't interested.

Then, during a grace-filled visit to Medugorje in 1995, our group traveled to see Fr. Jozo Zovko at his parish church St. Elijah's, in Tihaljina. While praying quietly in the church, I was startled by a woman who entered the pew behind me and tapped my shoulder. She asked me in English, "Do you have a brother?"

"Why, yes," I replied. Then she said, "I have a message for you. Our Lady says, 'Your brother will be fine.'" Immediately tears welled up in my eyes. This was so unexpected, so unexplainable, but so wonderful. During the journey back to Medjugorje, I was unable to speak from sheer happiness. Tears and a choking feeling filled my eyes and throat.

After returning to my community, I received a phone call from my brother. He asked, "Steve, do you really think an annulment is a possibility?" I told him, "I think so, but you won't know unless you try." I directed him to a priest in his city who could help him. He submitted his case to the diocesan marriage tribunal. Within less than two years it was decided that his first marriage was invalid. By August of 1997, my brother was received back into the sacramental life of the Church. And, in 1998, his wife was received into the Church at the Easter Vigil.

Before he received the annulment, my brother wrote, "The greatest void in my life is not being able to receive the Sacraments because of my divorce and remarriage. There is nothing in this world that I desire more than to have our marriage blessed by the Church, and to once again be accepted as a member with all the privileges of receiving the Sacraments."

After he was received back, he wrote to me, "I want to thank you, Steve, for all that you have done for us, your prayers, your encouragement, your love, and the fact that you never gave up. Because of you, I will be receiving my First Communion in many years. ...I thank God for allowing me to live long enough to see this dream come true. I will be ever grateful to you for the rest of my days. Thanks again, and please never stop praying for us." Isn't intercessary prayer powerful! Isn't God wonderful!

(End of Brother Stephen's story.)

After Sunday breakfast at Ivan's house, we asked questions, and Ivan explained about those first days and his fears of Our Lady and also the police. After all, the Communist government was in control then. I chided Ivan, saying, "How could you be afraid of Our Lady and of the police when you have Her protection?" I got my answer awfully quick. I'll be more careful after this.

On Sunday evening, immediately after the apparition, Ivan stood up, walked directly toward me and said, "I need to speak to you privately." We walked outside together and he said very bluntly, in his best broken "English," Tuesday night, Our Lady will have a message for you. She will give it to me right after the regular apparition."

WHOA!!!! I did not respond. I did not question. I was paralyzed. Then I began to wonder...what have I done? Today is Sunday. I now must wait two days. You mean She is too busy. I thought back and I had mistakenly thought we were the best of friends, and now She is going to remind me of all the times I totally ignored Her. She witnessed my every sin, I thought: now comes the day of reckoning.

I tried to remember every sin I ever committed, and I even came up with some new ones. Then I wondered, did I forget to confess something? I will tell you, I went through two nights of torture...Sunday night, no sleep at all; Monday night, very, very little sleep. Now the count down.

All day Tuesday, this was all I could think, "I'm in a lot of trouble, otherwise why did Our Lady make me wait 48 hours?" Then it was Tuesday evening and time for the apparition. I have never sweat more in my life, in such a short time. I thought that everybody goes through this when they die, but I am going through this in broad daylight. When the apparition is over, Ivan finishes writing and then hands me the verdict, I thought. He wrote in Croation, handed me the paper and said, "My English not good enough. You have to get translated."

Well, I couldn't read a thing, but I thought, at least the paper didn't burn my fingers. The next day, I got the translation. Wow, what a relief. In one short message, She displayed Her support, protection, love, and compassion.

The next day, Ivan and Laureen told me that they would like me to be the Godfather of their first child. Someone asked Laureen, "Why do you, from Boston, and Ivan from Medjugorje, ask someone from Iowa, not a relative, to be sponsor of your first child?" Laureen replied, "Because I know he will pray for our child." Ivan also told me that he wanted to ask me, but it was Laureen's idea. I was overwhelmed by this time, and I needed to return home for a rest.

Above: Brother Stephen at St. James Church in Medjugorje

Above: Sister Marie Louise on Cross Mountain in Medjugorje

Below: Sr. Marie Louise, Dragica, Marinko, and Br. Stephen in Medjugorje. Note pictures of visionaries in background

Above: Brother Stephen and George in Medjugorje
Below: Iran and Brother Stephen

Chapter 7

A Speaking Engagement

Life, it seems, has slowed but only for a couple of months. More people have become aware of my friendship with Ivan. Once, someone who was a total stranger, waited for me outside the chapel door. He approached me, and said, "Are you the person who is a friend of a visionary from Medjugorje?"

"Probably so," I answered. "Then, how does a person like me get to meet or speak to, or just see him?" he asked. I told him to write his name and address and phone number on a small piece of paper, and when Ivan comes I would see what I could do.

Soon, I realized that more people than I could fit into my house would like an experience with Ivan. I wondered where I could find a larger location. I know Ivan will appear anywhere I ask, so I didn't tell him. He always told me, "Everybody is welcome...more is better."

I called a local Monsignor who had experienced Medjugorje, and I told him that I needed a bigger room for Ivan to appear.

He said, "I have some connections at the local college. Let me see what is available." He called back and said that they have this room which can be expanded to hold a couple of hundred. I told him that I thought we needed something bigger, and he informed me, "It is better to fill a smaller room, than have a bigger room half filled." I think he could tell I felt we needed something really big. He then suggested the college theater. I told him that I would take that, if I couldn't find something bigger.

I then contacted a man with some experience in this line, and this man suggested Five Flags. I said, "I don't know anything about that place." He said, "Do you want me to get all the information? But, realize you only have about three weeks. I don't know what is available, and how will people know about it!"

I just told him, "Our Lady will handle it." He called back very soon, and said, "The night you want is wide open. The theater holds 650, and the arena can be opened to hold, I think, if I remember correctly, about 5000." I told him we would take both. He wanted to know if I was going to charge admission, and told him, "No way. I will print tickets and give them to whoever wants to come. That way we'll have an idea how to plan."

I called the Monsignor and told him everything. I told him that we can go to the theater first and then put the overflow into the arena, or fill the arena first and then go to the theater. We'll see how the tickets go. A couple of days later, I had the tickets. We called it "A Night With Ivan." Then the Monsignor called and suggested we ask Rita

Klaus to come and speak, also. I asked him why, and he said, "She has a great story, and she has roots in Dubuque."

I wanted to know what kind of roots, and he told me that her Grandfather was from Dubuque. I said to him, "You know it is just one evening. I don't know if we have time, but I'll see." He then said, "I have this great friend who has a great devotion to Our Lady, and I told her, 'You are always doing me favors. Now, maybe I can do one for you. Ivan is coming to Dubuque. Would you like to meet him?' and she replied, 'Yes, and as my gift to Our Lady, may I do all the advertising?' Her husband owns the local AM-FM radio station."

Her husband told me later that he would also announce this on seven sister stations around the area. In just a few days, all the tickets were gone, and I was asked, "What do we do now?" I said, "No problem," and ordered 3000 more tickets.

The manager of Five Flags found out about this and called me to warn me—maybe scold me would be a better word. She said, "Our capacity is 5000. I understand you will have 6000 tickets out, and I can assure you that we will monitor this closely because we have fire regulations, and when we reach capacity, the doors will be locked." I said, "OK, but Our Lady will control everything."

The man I called first was taking care of all the arrangements of Five Flags...a lady the Monsignor called was doing all the advertising...and a florist from Dickeyville asked if she could do all the floral arrangements. (She did a super job.) Many volunteers handled the crowd. I really did none of the work. I made a few phone calls. I never left my desk. Everything fell together so quickly and so smoothly, and I can't take any credit because I knew there was a hidden force behind all of it.

The person who was to interpret for Ivan told me directly, "You have no experience. You don't know what you are doing, and you are doing it all wrong." (The Monsignor thought this very humorous.) I couldn't argue with her. It was too late to change anything, and I had never done anything like this before. I was so inexperienced, I didn't know what to fear. To me it was a kind of natural high, and I had no goals except to fill Five Flags.

As to the Rita Klaus situation, which I was not really in favor of, I left it up to Our Lady. I looked at a statue of Our Lady, and said, "Hey, Mary, if you want Rita Klaus here, you make her available. If you don't want Rita Klaus here, you make her unavailable."

We had ten days until Ivan's appearance at Five Flags. I didn't know where Rita Klaus lived, so I called Chicago where I knew she had appeared at a Marian Conference. I asked them if they knew where Rita Klaus lived and they told me they did and gave me her phone number. I dialed this number, and her husband answered the phone. I asked if Rita was available to speak to me.

She came to the phone, and I said, "You probably don't know who I am, and that is not important, but where do you expect to be on November 16?" She replied, "On November 16, I will be driving to Dubuque, Iowa."

I wanted to know why, and she said, "I am originally from Waterloo, Iowa, and I'll be visiting there, and on the morning of November 16, I will be driving with my sister to visit my aged grandmother, whom I haven't seen for a long, long time."

I asked, "Did you know Ivan Dragicevic will be here?" She said, "No, maybe I will get to see him." I asked, "Would you help us out?" She replied, "George, I'll do anything you ask." This entire arrangement took less than 15 minutes. I then said, "Hey, Mary, I get the message."

The end result, I can tell you, is that I am very grateful to Rita Klaus. She was a huge contributor to that night. I am now a big fan of Rita's. I just love her dearly.

On November 16, I picked Ivan up at the airport, about noon. We greeted each other, and he immediately said, "The Blessed Mother is very happy about tonight...over 4000 people." I was stunned about Our Lady's happiness, but I thought, "Ivan, you're wrong about 4000 people. I expect 5000. After all, 6000 tickets were picked up."

That night I felt terribly unhappy because the place didn't fill up, and they had turned people away who didn't have tickets when the doors were first opened. I was unhappy for both those reasons, until Ivan handed me a message from Our Lady which had been given to him before the event, in which She said to be happy and to give Her all the difficulties.

Also, the husband doing the advertising, mentioned to me that he had been involved with the building and construction, and he estimated the crowd at slightly over 4000. Imagine that!

Ivan has been my closest friend for some time now, and probably always will be as long as I am around.

Above: Sign outside the Five Flags Center in Dubuque

Above: Rita Klaus
Below: Ivan and George

Chapter 8

The Mysterious Is Normal

Ivan has left now, and people have dispersed. I received a lot of mail from those that were at Five Flags. Ivan and Rita Klaus left their mark on a lot of people. Today, 6 years later, people still come up to me, and say, "I was at that 'Night With Ivan.' Can I tell you what happened to me?"

I received a call from a Mennonite who said that his wife told him she had no problem believing the words of Rita or Ivan. She believed every word and believed from the very beginning.

Very shortly, after this great evening, someone handed me a booklet entitled, "Rosary Meditations from Mother Teresa." I thought this was the most powerful little booklet that I ever came in contact with, and I thought everybody should have a copy of it. I saw where to get this: Apostolate of Perpetual Adoration, Fr. Martin Lucia, SS.CC.

I have felt for some time now that Perpetual Adoration of the Blessed Sacrament is the most important and moving tool of our faith. I called information and got the number, and when they answered, I inquired about purchasing some of these booklets. Pat Forton answered the phone and asked me how many I would need.

I told her I would like 1000. She just said, "Oh, my." I asked her what was the matter, and she told me I could get a special price, so I made it 2000. I think, overall, I ended up closer to 5000. She was quite impressed.

I asked her, "What do you do?" She told me she was Fr. Lucia's secretary for his ministry to promote Perpetual Adoration. I had a pleasant conversation with her, as she told me about their work. She also told me about Fr. Martin Lucia, who in November 1994, gave communion to Julia Kim in Hawaii.

The Eucharist turned to Flesh and Blood in Julia's mouth. She said, "I will send you a 16-page paper on the messages of Our Lady through Julia, featuring descriptions and pictures of Fr. Lucia and Julia Kim."

Now, I am not totally stupid, but at that moment I became an instant believer, fan, supporter, and follower of Julia Kim. I cannot deny this, and hinder Our Lady's mission. I know this is not the work of Satan.

Our Lady and the Eucharist are at the center of all activities in Naju, Korea, where Julia lives. I have read all of Our Lady's messages to the world through Julia many times. Whenever I read her messages, I always feel Our Lady is speaking directly to me...sort of like She is singling me out.

When I get in touch with something like this, I get so excited that I want to share it with the world. However, it seems it never affects others the same way. That is OK. I find Our Lady exciting, informative, prophetic, and fun. I enjoy Her prophecies. She tells you exactly what will happen.

I read the messages over again and decided I would really like to help spread Mary's messages. The article sent by Pat Forton had a name and phone number in the US, so I placed a call, and the conversation went like this: "Hello. Please, can you tell me, has there been any progress on building the church requested by Our Lady...the basilica Julia Kim was told to build on the mountains in Naju?"

She answered, "No." I asked, "Why?" She said, "Two reasons, 1) Julia do not have the money, 2) Julia do not have permission. ...My mother-in-law died." I said, "Oh. I'm sorry." Then she said, "Sang is at the funeral home." I said, "I take it, Sang is your husband?"

"Yes."

"And, this is his Mother?"

"Yes. He is making funeral arrangements." She said, "Can you call back in an hour or two?" I said, "No way, but maybe in a few days." She said, "OK."

I do not remember giving her my name or what I wanted. I know I did not give her a phone number. I found out a year later that he had no caller I.D., but four days later, my private phone, an unlisted number, rang, and when I answered the phone, I heard, "Sang Lee here. You wanted to talk to me." ...I am amazed but nothing seems normal any more, or like it used to be. The mysterious is normal.

I questioned his position in the events in Naju, and was impressed with his willingness to answer any questions I had. The trouble was, I didn't know much, so I couldn't ask a lot of questions. Early in the conversation he said, "Do you want to meet Julia?" I said, "Yes, but I don't know how that could be possible."

He replied, "You come to Oregon. I take you." My answer was, "I don't know." I thought, with my heart and Korea, the chances would be too great. He said, "Think about it and keep in touch." I sent a small donation to help him with his newsletter.

Now things seemed to be moving so quickly. In November—a Night With Ivan. In December—contact with Fr. Lucia and information on Julia. In January—contact with Sang Lee.

Then in February, I got a call from someone from St. Mary's Church in Dubuque, Iowa. The message was that the carpet was loose and could we come and fix it? I would try because, if it is pulled away from the wall, we can put it back but that was not the problem, however. Here is the problem:

Seven steps and two large pillars, with clover leaf shape—not 4 leaf but 6 leaf. We had originally installed this over 20 years ago. The wear was very good except it had stretched so badly, they were afraid they would trip over it. We had been called over a year before and I sent our layers, but I stayed in the office.

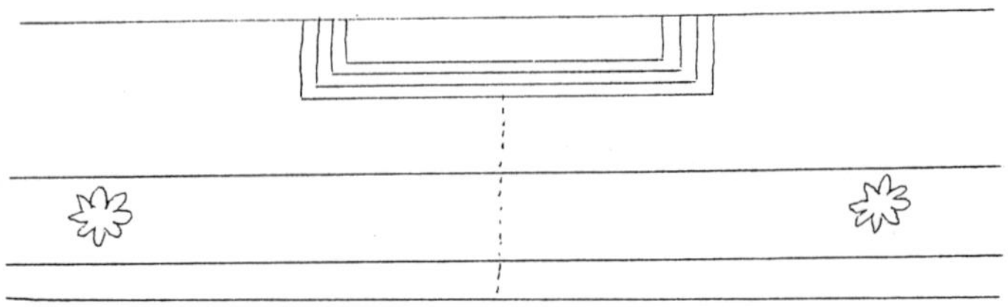

When, after a day, they came back I asked them how they did. They told me, "Terrible!" I asked if they had done their best, and when they told me, "Yes, but it is impossible." I said, "I can't ask for more."

Now, I get this new call and I decided to go with them. We went after early morning Mass. One of the most experienced layers said to me, "I think I know where all the black is coming from." I had assumed it was from people's feet because it was dirtiest where people walked. He said, "That pad under there is petroleum based, and I think it has deteriorated and the oil is coming up through the carpet." I said, "Well, we can steam clean it, maybe."

We were standing under the statue of the Immaculate Heart of Mary, the three of us. I happened to look up and it was an instantaneous response. I said, "Last time you tried to correct this, it didn't work. This time we'll ask for Her help." I was looking up at the statue. I said, "This is Her house. This is St. Mary's." I am not smart enough to think of something like this or to say something like this but, even though the layers didn't say anything, it was clear that their inner reaction was, "Good idea."

Then one of the layers asked, "What do you want us to do?" I told them to remove the carpet from the top step which was not difficult at all. The pad was dried and it totally broke into pieces when we went to pick it up. We replaced it with new padding and put the carpet back, stretched it and trimmed the excess. The oldest layer stood up and said, "Look at this." His jeans had turned black where his knees were in contact with the carpet. His tan scuffed shoes also turned black.

I told the layers to go to the next step and then the next step. When they got down four steps they wanted to know what else to do. They knew the pillars would be a big problem because the carpet stretched so much that there would be a hole along side each pillar. I told them to cut it down the middle. They said, "You mean, stretch it from the pillars to the middle?" I told them, "Yes."

They said, "Do you realize this is a pattern piece of goods and won't match in the middle?" I replied, "Yes, I know. But we have no choice." Again, there was no way that I could think of this by myself. I am not a carpet layer. Somebody had to put this idea in my head. Stretching this to the center, making nice straight cuts, and putting it together is a very exacting task.

Friday night, the job was complete. It was nice and tight but the pattern was off and the surface was very oily. Then on Saturday morning, when I went to Mass there, I noticed that the carpet was perfectly clean! The seam was practically undetectable, but then I knew where it was! And, this morning the pattern matched!

I must tell about the first day on the job. I went to see the progress around 2 o'clock, and I was carrying a bag of lemon drops. I asked the layers if they would like a lemon drop because there was no water in the church for them. I said, "Here, take the whole bag." It was then that I noticed the younger layer had a lemon drop between his right thumb and forefinger. I said to him, "Are you looking to share a lemon drop with Our Lady?" He said, "I was thinking about it."

I told him, "Go ahead. People give Her roses. I guess you can share a lemon drop." The ledge of the platform where the statue of the Immaculate Heart of Mary stood is quite high, but by jumping, the young man was able to place the lemon drop there. I don't know what happened during the night. However, when the carpet became clean, the lemon drop was gone!

Chapter 9

The Investments Paid Off!

One day, I think in March, 1996 sometime, a sizable parcel arrived at my office. I noticed the sender, "Mary's Touch by Mail, Sang Lee." I opened it and inside was a replica statue of Juliza Kim's statue. I did not ask for it. I didn't even know if this was possible, but I placed it in my office on a server alongside of my desk. This is really neat, I felt. She is my favorite subject. I thought no more about it.

Now, my office door is always held open by a doorstop at night. I left the statue in my office. The next day I went to my desk. I am always aware when someone has been into my desk, or any of my files, or the bookcases, or the catalogues, or the papers on my desk. I don't mind, only this time I was certain that whoever had gone through everything in the office was not able to return things. I was wondering what was going on here last night. I then closed my door. Later, when I walked into my office after going out to the floor, I noticed a very nice aroma and I thought, "One of the girls was in here with a lot of perfume on."

By noon, all the girls were discussing the fragrance, and trying to find out where it was coming from. The men said the fragrance was so strong that it could be sensed out on the floor. "Oh," I thought. "So that explains what went on here last night." Then, I went directly to the statue and found that the fragrance came from the heart of the statue of Our Lady. Almost immediately, I called Sang Lee, and before I could say anything, he said, "You got the statue?

"Yes," I said, "but do you know what the statue is doing?" I thought that he must have had other experiences like this. He said, "No, how could I know? The statue is with you and I am in Oregon." I told him about the statue giving off a fragrance, quite strong I thought.

He replied, "I know of one other one that did that, but it didn't give the fragrance until Julia walked into the room." He then added, "Our Lady told Julia that whenever this happens, it is a sign that She, the Blessed Mother, is in your presence, and you are receiving special graces." In my heart I said, "Thank you, Sang Lee. Thank you, Julia." Sang told me that Julia had prayed over this statue.

At this time, I was reading the book, "In The Kingdom Of The Spirit" by Joseph Terelya. As usual, after reading this book, I felt many people should read it. Inside the cover was printed, published by Abba House, along with a telephone number. I wanted to order some copies, so I called.

The phone rang quite a while before a woman answered. I asked, “Is this the Abba House?” She answered, “No. I live next door and when they can't answer, the call transfers to my house.” I asked her who she was and she told me, “Geraldine Carrigan.” This meant nothing to me, so I asked her what her connection was with Abba House.

She told me that Bishop Danylak had translated the book, “In The Kingdom Of The Spirit,” and that she had edited it. I said, “So how did you know Bishop Danylak? Are you Ukrainian?” She said, “No, I have been a missionary for many years in the Far East. I speak Japanese.” I asked, “Are you Japanese?” She laughed, “No, can't you tell by the name? I am Irish.”

“Well,” I said, “Women have ways of changing their names.” She said, “That is not the case here.” The conversation continued, and I asked, “Do you know Sr. Sasakawa from Akita, Japan?” She did not, but wished she did, and then she added that she had become quite knowledgeable about Julia Kim. I again thought, “Isn't this amazing?”

Geraldine told me she was presently working on publishing a paper, “Heart of the Harvest” which explains the Eucharistic Miracle at Naju at a Mass celebrated by Bishop Roman Danylak. I asked when it would be ready, and when she told me she had a problem of being short of funds, I told her I would have it in the mail to her within the hour. “Hey, Mary, this is for the one I owe You.”

Geraldine asked me if she should inform Bishop Danylak what I was doing. I told her that my name would mean nothing to him, and besides it is for the Blessed Mother and

She knows. But, I told her I would like some copies.

I received the papers in April, about 25 of them, of which I still have one copy that I want to keep for myself. I still remain in close contact with Geraldine and Sang Lee. This has never been a chore. My relationship with these people is a total joy, and I get regular calls from my very good friend, Ivan, also.

I really wanted to help the Blessed Mother more. However, I didn't have the means. One day in July, I went to the chapel, before the exposed Eucharist , and said, “Hey, Mary...I'll make You a deal. I have some commodity positions (like She didn't know), and here is what I'll do. I have positions in coffee, cocoa, beans, and silver. I will not trade them. I'll only keep them until they expire. Now, I know Mary, You have no money, so if they lose, I'll have to cover the losses, but the gains I will give to You to spread Your messages through Julia Kim. Is this OK?”

Mary has never spoken to me where I could hear Her, but She didn't say no, so I guessed it was all right. I told two people about it— my ex-partner, and my oldest co-worker. I tried to explain to Sang Lee, but he informed me he didn't want to be involved because this was between the Blessed Mother and myself.

The two people I told this to could not believe what was happening. I gladly told them and now include a copy of the trans- actions for all my readers to see. All the positions were closed on November 8, 1996. I told Her, “Hey, Mary...$74,841.19!” I was so grateful to Her, but I would never advise anyone to do this. It had never worked for me before, and I never tried anything like this again. Here are copies of the transactions:

Made Promise 7-26-96

			CONFIRMATION				DATE -	7/16/96
7/16/96		1	SEPT96 NYFE COMPOSITE INDEX UNSOLICITED	R	33030			
7/16/96	2		SEPT96 NYFE COMPOSITE INDEX UNSOLICITED	R	33700			
			PURCHASE AND SALE					
7/16/96	2		SEPT96 NYFE COMPOSITE INDEX	D	33700			
7/16/96		1	SEPT96 NYFE COMPOSITE INDEX	D	33030			
7/15/96		1	SEPT96 NYFE COMPOSITE INDEX	R	34675			
			P&S					1,525.00
			COMMISSIONS				117.00	
			FEES				4.28	
			**TOTAL P&S					1,525.00
			**TOTAL FEES				117.00 4.28	
			**NET P&L					[illegible]
			Gained $50.86 OPEN POSITIONS		7-26-96			
7/15/96	5		DEC96 CBT CORN	R	375			
			OPEN TRADE EQUITY		367 1/4	3.17	387.50	-2900.00
7/03/96	5		NOV96 CBT BEANS	R	742 1/2			
			OPEN TRADE EQUITY		793 1/2	7.28	-725.00	2,550.00
7/05/96	5		NOV96 CBT BEANS	R	730			
			Gained $9677.58 OPEN TRADE EQUITY		793 1/2	7.28	-100.00	3,175.00
7/15/96	5		NOV96 CBT BEANS	R	799			
			OPEN TRADE EQUITY		793 1/2	7.28	275.00	3550.00
	15		TOTAL FOR COMMODITY					5,450.00
6/11/96	1		DEC96 COMEX SILVER	R	53000			
			Lost $1334.14 OPEN TRADE EQUITY		50230	5.06	1,385.00	-1200.00
6/20/96	1		DEC96 NCS COCOA	R	1431			
			Lost $669.14 OPEN TRADE EQUITY		1377	13.96	540.00	-350
6/11/96	1		DEC96 NCS COFFEE	R	11410			
			Gained $15350.49 OPEN TRADE EQUITY		9805	97.00	6,018.75	-6412.50
7/01/96	1		DEC96 NCS COFFEE	R	11400			
			OPEN TRADE EQUITY		9805	97.00	5,981.25	-6375.00
	2		TOTAL FOR COMMODITY				12,000.00	
			ACCOUNT BALANCE					
			***TOTAL OPEN TRADE EQUITY				8,862.50	-$21612.50
			***LEDGER BAL					20,110.46
[redacted] INC.			Gained $23075.63					11,247.96
			***TOTAL EQUITY					17,108.41

Made Promise 7-26 96

Acct #1 Gain +$23,075.63
acct #2 Gain +$23,075.63
acct #3 Gain + $28,689.93

Total Gain $74,841.19

Finished November 8, 1996

Promise 7-26-96

Date	Qty		Description		Price		Amount	Handwritten
			P&S				1,525.00	
			COMMISSIONS			117.00		
			FEES			4.28		
							1,525.00	
						117.00		
							[illegible]03.72	
7/1[illegible]					375			3.17
					367 1/4	387.50		—2900.00
5/2[illegible]					773			7.28
					793 1/2		1,025.00	—2250.00
5/28/96	5		NOV96 CBT BEANS	R	779			7.28
			OPEN TRADE EQUITY		793 1/2		[illegible]25.00	—2550.00
7/05/96	5		NOV96 CBT BEANS	R	730			7.28
			OPEN TRADE EQUITY		793 1/2		3,175.00	—1[illegible]
7/15/96	5		NOV96 CBT BEANS	R	799			7.28
			OPEN TRADE EQUITY		793 1/2	275.00		—3550
	20		TOTAL FOR COMMODITY				4,650.00	
4/30/96	1		SEPT96 COMEX SILVER	R	54150			4.99½
			OPEN TRADE EQUITY		49430	2,360.00		—2100.00
5/21/96	1		SEPT96 COMEX SILVER	R	53550			4.99½
			OPEN TRADE EQUITY		49430	2,060.00		—1800.00
5/23/96	1		SEPT96 COMEX SILVER	R	54100			4.99½
			OPEN TRADE EQUITY		49430	2,335.00		—2075.00
	3		TOTAL FOR COMMODITY			6,755.00		
6/11/96	1		DEC96 COMEX SILVER	R	53000			5.06½
			OPEN TRADE EQUITY		50230	1,385.00		—1175.00
6/14/96	1		SEPT96 NCS COCOA	R	1462			closed out at 949.14
			OPEN TRADE EQUITY		1339	1,230.00		13.58 —1040.00
6/20/96	1		DEC96 NCS COCOA	R	1431			13.96
			OPEN TRADE EQUITY		1377	540.00		—350.00
6/11/96	1		DEC96 NCS COFFEE	R	11400			97.00
			OPEN TRADE EQUITY		9805	5,981.25		—6375.00
7/01/96	1		DEC96 NCS COFFEE	R	11400			97.00
			OPEN TRADE EQUITY		9805	5,981.25		—6375.00
	2		TOTAL FOR COMMODITY			11,962.50		

Gained $12,903.44

Gained $2322.58

Lost 1359.14

Gained $90.86

Lost $669.14

Gained $15350.47

Total Gained $28,689.93

	***TOTAL OPEN TRADE EQUITY	17,610.00	
GEORGE H. BANWORTH		—32,640.00	
	***LEDGER BAL		34,718.41
	***TOTAL EQUITY		17,108.41

40

Made Promise 7-26-96

CONFIRMATION

Date	Long	Short	Description		Price		Debit	Credit
							DATE -	7/16/96
7/16/96		1	SEPT96 NYFE COMPOSITE INDEX UNSOLICITED	R	33030			
7/16/96	2		SEPT96 NYFE COMPOSITE INDEX UNSOLICITED	R	33700			

7-26-96 - $75827.50

PURCHASE AND SALE

Date	Long	Short	Description		Price		Debit	Credit
7/16/96	2		SEPT96 NYFE COMPOSITE INDEX	D	33700			
7/16/96		1	SEPT96 NYFE COMPOSITE INDEX	D	33030			
7/15/96		1	SEPT96 NYFE COMPOSITE INDEX	R	34675			
			P&S					1,525.00
			COMMISSIONS				117.00	
			FEES				4.28	
			**TOTAL P&S					1,525.00
			**TOTAL COMMISSIONS				117.00	
			**TOTAL FEES				4.28	
			**NET P&L					1,403.72

Gained $5086 — 7-26-96

OPEN POSITIONS

Date	Long	Short	Description		Price	Handwritten	Debit	Credit
7/15/96	5		DEC96 CBT CORN OPEN TRADE EQUITY	R	375 367 1/4	3.17	387.50	-2900.00
7/03/96	5		NOV96 CBT BEANS OPEN TRADE EQUITY	R	742 1/2 793 1/2	7.28 -725.00		2,550.00
7/05/96	5		NOV96 CBT BEANS OPEN TRADE EQUITY	R	730 793 1/2	7.28 -100.00		3,175.00
7/15/96	5		NOV96 CBT BEANS OPEN TRADE EQUITY	R	799 793 1/2	7.28 - 3550.00	275.00	
	15		TOTAL FOR COMMODITY					5,450.00
6/11/96	1		DEC96 COMEX SILVER OPEN TRADE EQUITY	R	53000 50230	5.06	1,385.00	-1200.00
6/20/96	1		DEC96 NCS COCOA OPEN TRADE EQUITY	R	1431 1377	13.96	540.00	-350.00
6/11/96	1		DEC96 NCS COFFEE OPEN TRADE EQUITY	R	11400 9805	97.00	5,981.25	-6375.00
7/01/96	1		DEC96 NCS COFFEE OPEN TRADE EQUITY	R	11400 9805	97.00	5,981.25	-6375.00
			TOTAL FOR COMMODITY				11,962.50	

Gained $9677.58

Lost $1334.14

Lost $669.14

Gained $15,350.47

BANWORTH-UDELHOVEN, INC.
P.O. Box 637
DUBUQUE, IA 52004-0637

Date	Long			
1/18/96	60			

Total Gain $23075.63

$21575.00

ACCOUNT BALANCE

	Debit	Credit
***TOTAL OPEN TRADE EQUITY	8,825.00	
***LEDGER BAL		4,267.02
***TOTAL EQUITY	4,557.98	
		17,108.41

BANWORTH-UDELHOVEN

Chapter 10

A Lesson From A Bird

Somebody told me about a movement called Divine Will. The papers on this were written by Luisa Piccarreta. I went overboard about this again and, I think, I purchased fifteen sets of videos and about six to ten sets of the books, which consist of thirty volumes to a set. I found the videos most interesting and the books quite difficult to understand, but I wanted so desperately to understand.

Just don't tell me what I may believe. This person, Luisa Piccarreta, lived over sixty years on the Eucharist—no food and no drink. I can judge this for myself. I have read all her writings, all thirty books. I admit they were much too deep for me. However, one cannot read thirty books on one subject without getting something out of them. I am a believer. Also, Luisa Piccarreta has now been beatified.

I do know that the people I gave these videos and books to never followed through and read any, or very little. There is one exception, and you know who you are. It is much easier to be a skeptic than to study something like this. Personally, I think some day in the not too far distant, everyone will know about this and many people will live in "His Divine Will." I do not mean doing His will, because if I do His will, that is still my will. Living in His will is totally giving up my will.

One day, I received an early morning phone call from a co-worker from the Quad-cities. I detected that this person was somewhat down, and I asked, "Why so gloomy?" She just said, "My pet bird got away." I thought, "Be glad, not sad," but I asked her what kind of bird it was. She said, "It was a cockatiel. You know, one time you called my house and you said you had difficulty hearing me and asked me who was being so rude to be yelling in the background. Well, this is the same one." I said, "I do not even know what a cockatiel is."

I was informed that the bird is golden in color and about twelve inches from beak to end of tail, that she is tropical and she needs to be kept out of a draft. I asked, "How could you lose a bird this size?" My co-worker said, "She was riding on my shoulder and my front door bell rang, and when I opened the door, she flew out into a tree and would not come back."

It was late winter, early spring, and below freezing at night so, of course, she was worried. They had had the whole neighborhood watching this bird. They put ladders up the tree and were even on the roof of the house, trying to reach her. Whenever anyone got close, she would just fly a little further away. They even called the fire department, who responded, but had no success. I asked, "Where is the bird now?" She said, "She is in a neighbor's tree and my neighbor is watching her for me." I asked her to keep me informed about the bird after she went home to lunch.

When lunch was over, she called me back. "She is a little further away now. I don't think she will be able to live now. We have snow flurries forecast for tonight." I called her at 4:50 and asked, "What is the latest on your bird?" She said, "She is gone. We live very close to Highway 280, a bypass around Davenport. All the trees are cut so you have this clear area from our neighborhood, and then some distance away, maybe 1000 feet, there is a forest. My neighbor saw her fly across the clear area, and she flew into the forest. By now, if she is not dead, she is lost anyway." I told her she could get another bird just like the one that flew away, but she said, "It just wouldn't be the same."

I left the office to make my usual trip to the chapel and, when I went before the exposed Blessed Sacrament, I said, "Hey, Mary, give her back the bird. It isn't going to hurt anything, and something good might come out of it." That is all I said, not another word.

I need to explain. This person in Davenport often called herself an agnostic. Very little contact with any church, but she often heard me speak of Our Lady, and knows I have a lot of concern for her soul and her need to convert.

The next morning, after my chapel visit, I received a phone call from this lady, very serious and very subdued. Before she could say anything, I said, "You got the bird back!" She said, "Yes, and as soon as it was back, I just knew you had something to do with it, and I thank you."

I asked her how the bird came back and she said, "A neighbor brought her back. I told you, the entire neighborhood knew about this bird. She had flown to a neighbor's tree and somehow he lured her into his trap. He brought her back this morning." I asked her if the bird seemed happy to be back and she told me, "No. She refuses to look at me. Whenever I get close, she turns the opposite direction."

What she said next just about floored me. She said, "I know one thing. God controls the birds. They do just exactly what He tells them. He can't do anything with people, because they have a free will." I thought to myself that she has a better understanding about Divine Will than most churchgoers.

I told her about my part in all this, which was very little, and she thanked me again and was ready to sign off, but I said, "Oh no; now you have got to pay the price." She was agreeable. I told her she must say five words, three times a day. When she asked for how long, I just said to say these five words, three times a day. When she had gotten paper and pencil to write them down, I said, very slowly, "Holy——Mary——— Mother——of———God——." She said, "Is that it?" I said, "Yes, that's it. Remember, not in a hurry." She understood, but wanted to know if she had to say these words out loud, or could she think them. I told her that either way would be OK.

About three weeks later, I asked this person, "Did you remember to say those five words every day?" She told me she had said them every day but one, but made up for that on the next day. I said, "Fine, now you are ready for five more words." Very slowly I said, "Pray——for——us—— sinners——now——."

"NOW!" she said, quite strongly, "Isn't that being kind of demanding?" I told her I was sure Our Blessed Mother doesn't mind. She will be happy to hear from her. Some time later she informed me that she had learned the end of these ten words, and when I asked her from whom, she said she heard it on TV.

Some months went by. I had reason to go to the Davenport store with another person. I was to go about mid-morning when I got a phone call from this same lady who inquired, “Haven’t you left yet?” I asked her if I needed to hurry, but she just wanted me to know that there was someone waiting for me there. I arrived about an hour and a half later. As I walked towards the office, I asked her, “Who wants to see me?”

She told me to just go into the office as she is waiting in there. I walked in and to my complete surprise, there stood this bird. Not in a cage. Totally free to fly anywhere in this building which is 100' x 300', a very large area.

This bird flexed her wings and truly frightened me, but I was told, “Go up to her and put out your forefinger for a perch.” I did so, very reluctantly. The bird walked onto my finger and then up my left arm to my shoulder, then around on my back to the right shoulder and rubbed her head under my right earlobe.

The bird stayed right there for about three hours. When I moved, she went right with me. I got to really like this bird. I thought that the bird was very affectionate. This bird taught me something about His Divine Will.

It was right about this time that Brother Stephen informed me that he was leaving to begin studies for the priesthood. He told me he had discerned to become a priest while in Medjugorje. To me it was a joyous message. He said it would take two years to complete his studies.

Above: George and the bird
Below: George and the bird showing affection

Ordination
to the Priesthood
Stephen Verbest, O.C.S.O.

August 15, 1998
Solemnity of the Assumption

we praise you
we bless you
we worship you
we glorify you

Above: Praise God! Steven becomes a priest

Chapter 11

Meeting With Julia Kim

Some time later, Sang Lee called to inform me that Julia Kim would be coming to California later in 1997, and he felt I must make the trip. I told him I would try, but I can never plan too far in the future. I am not that sure of the future.

When the time came closer, I decided to try to go to California and so on Thursday, November 6, 1997, we were scheduled to leave Moline, Illinois at 7 a.m., but no TWA plane! So, we changed to United and left a half hour earlier. We were barely in the air when I felt chest discomfort. I knew what this was, since I had a lot of experience.

I said, "Hey, Mary, not here and not now. Wait until I get home." It passed quickly. We arrived at the Los Angeles airport one and a half hours early, but at a different terminal building, which meant walking and taking a shuttle bus, finally arriving at the TWA location where I had told Sang Lee to meet us, still a half hour ahead of schedule.

Sang Lee and Father Francis Su both came to the airport to greet us, and what a greeting! After many contacts with Sang by both phone and mail, this was the first personal meeting. Imagine, after a year and some months, we finally meet.

Father Su explained, "We are one in Spirit, with the same goals, all arranged by Our Lady, united in one family with Julia to strive to spread the messages as given to her." Father Su continued, "I feel so privileged to have been present at three Eucharistic miracles."

We walked arm in arm leaving this area and, walking again, came to Air Canada to pick up Bishop Danylak.

I had learned to respect and admire Sang Lee over a period of time, and my feeling for Father Su matched those feelings instantly, as Father Su showed immediate love and affection. Getting to know Bishop Danylak took somewhat longer.

Now, Bishop Danylak joined the group, along with my companion, Charlie, and we headed for the parking ramp. I walked hand in hand with Father Su. Father Su said that Bishop Danylak is now also of this family and suggested maybe he, Father Su, could just be Bishop Danylak's humble altar boy. I suggested I am just the "uncle." Father Su liked the idea that this Gentile was his "uncle." He later added the other Gentile as "Uncle Charlie."

Sang headed to downtown Los Angeles toward our hotel, but first he stopped at a restaurant and asked us, "Korean, Chinese, or American?" Bishop Danylak suggested Korean, much to the delight of Sang and

Father Su. Upon entering, I looked at all the food and could identify nothing except the rice. It looked so good that I wanted it all. I found the largest plate and proceeded to take a very small amount of everything, which I learned is not a good idea.

When we arrived at our table, the waitress questioned, “What to drink?” I said, “Coffee.” She said, “No coffee...tea?” I said, “Skim milk.” She said, “No milk.” I said, “Any kind of milk.” She said, “No kind of milk.” I said, “Water?” She said “OK.”

There were no potatoes, no bread, and no utensils...just two sticks. What an experience! Charlie witnessed my struggle and said, “You have to eat it. You don't want to insult them.” Yeah, right! Sang and Father Su attacked the food with much vigor! I offered up my pain.

After much effort and just a little success, we headed for the hotel, arriving shortly after 3:00 p.m. Charlie wanted to take a shower but, after entering our room, I received a phone call. It was Sang asking us to be in the lobby in ten minutes. When I told Charlie, he said it was OK.

When we joined the others in the lobby, Sang said our destination was an hour drive. However, during rush hour it would probably be longer, especially since he doesn't know the area around Long Beach that well. Father Su measures the distance in Rosaries. Los Angeles downtown is one Rosary, highway time is three Rosaries, etc.

We arrived at our destination at about 6:15. Mass was to begin at 7:00 p.m. We were asked to await the arrival of Julia in the hall next to the Church. About 15 minutes later, Julia entered with the aid of two women, who had accompanied her from Naju.

Father Su informed me that she is suffering the pains of abortion at this time. Her stomach is swollen. I had never seen her before. Her knees buckled, but she was held up and helped to a sofa, and after a few minutes was too ill to sit up. During all this, her eyes were closed. Then the priest and Bishop were asked to visit, and I disappeared to the center of the Church surrounded by people. Sang went to the front pew to translate for Julia, and Uncle Charlie helped the Bishop and carried his vestments.

Bishop Danylak is of the Eastern Rite, Byzantine, more traditional, much less modern, and that appealed to me. Mass lasted until almost 8:15. Then Julia spoke, with translations in both English and Spanish. That made it quite lengthy, over two hours. Then she offered to pray over every person there. No one was forced to stay but no one left, even though the next day was a work day for them. I waited until the last, and Father Su said to Julia, "This my Uncle." Julia and I were both amused. It was now close to midnight.

We returned from this Church in Long Beach, to our hotel in downtown Los Angeles. As we were getting close to our hotel, Sang informed us we were to give Julia two minutes and then come to her room. We did that and guess what? After a most warm and loving reception from Julia, two volunteers arrived with two huge boxes which contained a repeat of the meal we had about two hours earlier, from the same restaurant. Bishop Danylak begged off because he was exhausted, and

Charlie took his to his room because he needed to take some medicine. Yeah, right! I was the only Gentile with 16 Koreans. Yes, Charlie, you have to eat it. You don't want to insult them!

On Friday, November 7, 1997, I woke up sick. I mean really sick. Too sick to remain standing, and after a while, too sick to sit up. So I reclined on my bed after a bowl of oatmeal. Bishop came to the coffee shop as I was leaving to return to my room and he came with me. He could tell I was not well. He stayed several hours. I was lying on my bed and Bishop Danylak was sitting in a chair alongside. He is really precious. I now know ten swhy Our Lady had kind remarks for Bishop Danylak when he gave Communion to Julia that turned into His Flesh and Blood.

I have met a few Bishops, but none like this. This man was so simple, so ordinary, so kind, but so confident, so knowledgeable, so awesome. It was a reward to spend time with him. Thank you, Mary, for arranging all of this.

At one point, I asked him, “How do you get to meet all these fabulous people, like Joseph Terelya and Julia Kim and Pat Devlin and others?” He replied, “Well almost no one wants anything to do with them.” That is too bad for them. Then we discussed Geraldine Carrigan and at one point, I think, he decided I knew too much.

He looked directly into my eyes and said, “Are you that anonymous donor who helped Geraldine publish my testimony?” I had to smile and admit it. He then said, “How can anyone know who you are? You won't tell anybody who you are.” Oh yes, I DO-o-o-o-o-o!

The Bishop left and in walked Father Su. He prayed over me for 20 minutes with one hand on my forehead and holding my hand with his other. What a blessing to be sick. He remained a while, then I rested about two hours, until it was time to go to another Church and have a repeat of the night before.

This was a much bigger Church and even more crowded, with people standing down the side aisles and double down the middle aisle. Attendance was over 2000, I thought. Julia did not pray over the people, however. It would have been too late, but many people would not leave and they crowded around Julia.

I was in the back one-fourth of the church with Sang Lee, when someone tapped me on the arm and said, "Picture, Father, picture!" I said to Sang, "I am not a Priest!" He said, "Almost, so pose!" We both posed so he could take pictures.

We arrived back at the hotel quite late, but again Julia wanted everyone to come to her room for another great feast of Korean food. She just wanted everyone to share in her best. Again she was very warm, loving and kind. We retired about an hour earlier than the night before, because the next day was an all-day event.

On Saturday, November 8, 1997, we left for the Long Beach Convention Center at 8:00 a.m. We arrived after 9:00 a.m. with Mass at 10:00, followed by Adoration and a talk by Bishop Danylak about his experiences in Naju.

There was a break at 12:30, and it was then I met Sang Lee's wife. She is much like Sang, same mission in life, but she is so tiny. I later said, "Sang, she cannot weigh over 65 lb." He insisted that she weighed 90 lb. Her name is Heasook. She remembered very well our first conversation. She told me she thought the call came from Heaven, not because I sounded like God, but because she really expected to hear from Heaven because her mother-in-law, Sang's mother, had just died, and they expected to hear from someone. Sang's mother had passed away on July 27, 1996.

About two days later, Julia saw her in purgatory and urged him to offer more Masses. Then she dropped her head on my shoulder, a truly affectionate gesture. It was here that I asked Heasook about my first contact with her. I asked if she had given Sang my phone number. She said, "No. You called him back." But, I didn't. She knows I did not give her my number; I know that too, and Sang said he didn't know how he received my number. He said that it was too long ago to remember.

Later Julio, Julia's husband, spoke. He became a Catholic before Julia. He told about the bleeding statue with blood down the entire front and onto a table and then onto the floor. A considerable time later, about a couple of days after seeing the statue all bloody, he noticed that the table and the floor were clean. He checked with all the ladies and found out that no one had cleaned anything. Later, Our Lady told Julia that She had sent some angels to clean everything. At this point, in my own mind, the lights went on. Now I knew how the carpet at St. Mary's Church in Dubuque was cleaned.

After Julio spoke, Julia spoke. Then the day was complete except for trying to leave. Father Su and I were standing in the lobby area and were being surrounded by people wanting his blessing and wanting articles blessed. He couldn't refuse them, but did ask one person, “Didn't we already bless that inside?” She said, “No, I just purchased them.” Her husband asked, “Were these all blessed before they came here from Korea?” Father was blessing, so I said, “No, you may not sell blessed articles. They are blessed afterward.”

He then asked, “Are you the Bishop?” Father Su answered him, “No, he the Bishop Uncle. He higher than the Bishop.” Indeed, I was on the first step of the exit from the convention center. After finally getting out of there, we went to a Chinese restaurant. What a relief, but now I began feeling sadness because I knew this was our final meal together.

We left on Sunday, November 9, 1997. I felt like it had been a year since we left home. On the way, Sang said, “You should really think about going to Naju next year.” I said, “I will do whatever you ask.” He then said, “OK. Then you come to Naju three times. Next year, then again when start to build Basilica, then when Basilica is completed, facing the conversion of China.” I had no idea what that meant. I told him, “I don't think I will be around that long.” He told me, “You are not in control.”

Above: Father Su, George, and Sang Lee.
First meeting at the Los Angeles airport
Below: Father Su, Bishop Danylak, and Julia Kim
at the Los Angeles Conference

Above: Bishop Danylak, Julia Kim, and George
in Los Angeles

Chapter 12

A Visit To Naju, Korea

Sang Lee has written often, at least two times a month. He constantly makes me aware of the happenings in Naju, and our Blessed Mother's messages through Julia Kim. In Korea, there hasn't been much change. Even though the chapel has been completely left bare—no kneelers, no pews, no altar, only a small niche in the wall where Julia's statue of the Blessed Mother remains. This is where miracles happened...the shedding of tears and the Eucharist coming down and landing on the floor.

The following is an excerpt of a letter from Sang Lee: "Pilgrims continue coming to the chapel. They are amazed at the strong fragrance of roses from the spot on the floor where the Eucharist landed on August 27, 1997.

Julia is still in seclusion in her private quarters, praying, suffering, and trying to improve her health. Her doctor advised her to do some physical exercise. I think that is a very good idea. We hope that she will be much healthier by the time the official Church position is reversed.

Some people in Korea are excited, because two Eucharistic miracles that occurred to a 30-year-old woman in India last year are being recognized by the local Archbishop in India. As with Julia, the Sacred Host turned into visible flesh and blood in the lady's mouth. Koreans are asking why the same kind of Eucharistic miracles are approved in India and rejected in Korea."

Sang also wrote: "At this time, most of our shipments, not only to other countries, but to domestic destinations, are being sent free. I hope people's response will become stronger. We are not worried, because we know Our Lady will be victorious sooner or later.

"We have also been sending letters and articles to the Vatican and to all the bishops in Korea. The Archdiocese of Seoul, the capital city of Korea, now has a new Archbishop, Most Rev. Nicholaus Jin Suk Cheong. In comparison with his predecessor, Archbishop Cheong is said to be more loyal to the Church's teachings, and more favorable to Naju."

Sang Lee, his wife Heasook, and I decided to take our trip to Naju in October, 1998. On October 14, I went to be with Sang and Heasook for a short time. I arrived at Sang's house at 8:30 p.m. They served a meal of tofu soup, salad, pickled ginger, fish cake, North Korean pancakes (made from navy beans and the fruit of the bean sprouts), baked salmon, rice, seaweed, and ginseng tea. Also, we read a fax from Archbishop Bulaitis, former Vatican Pro Nuncio in Korea.

Our bags arrived at 7 a.m. the next day, October 15. At 7:30 a.m., we had about 2 oz. of spring water from Naju. Sang said they drink just a little every day. Then we read a fax from Father Spies. Heasook found out Korean food was not to my liking and she served oatmeal, corned beef hash, eggs, watermelon, milk, and coffee for breakfast.

As we were visiting, Sang expressed his opinion on chastisements. "The Church must be cleansed...the dogmas proclaimed...and Naju approved. We need that, for the conversion of the majority of Asia. Our Lady said She came to Korea because the majority of the Japanese did not heed Her messages."

We went to noon Mass at Holy Rosary Church, about 35 minutes away driving time. The priests are Dominicans. Two priests were hearing confessions when we arrived, which was about 30 minutes before Mass was scheduled to start. They continued to hear confessions all through the Mass. They have communion rails ever since the Church was established.

There was no hugging, no kissing, no socializing, no grabbing the Eucharist in the hand, no standing while receiving, no Eucharistic Ministers and, in my opinion, many times greater respect and devotion to the Eucharist. After Mass, exposition of the Blessed Sacrament took place. I was told it is like this every day and late into the night, interrupted only by the 5:30 p.m. Mass.

Sang said Oregon is bigger than Iowa and is the same size as North and South Korea. The population of Oregon is 3 million, about the same as Iowa, but North and South Korea has a population of 70 million. The people in Korea are always in a hurry, and the result is the highest automobile accident ratio in the world.

Sang Lee converted to Catholicism during his sophomore year in high school, though his Daddy was a Presbyterian minister. He said he converted because he wanted more than his own church, at that time, could give him. He said that it was reading the lives of the Saints that convinced him to become Catholic.

I asked him if his parents objected. He replied, “They were not happy about it, but they did not try to prevent it.” His parents' friends objected, however. “How could this son of a clergyman become Catholic?” Sang's wife, Heasook, and Julia and Julio all converted from the same faith.

Sang told me, his mother went to Mass with him daily for five years before she converted. It was very hard for her, being the wife of a minister. Sang's older brother is a Presbyterian minister also, and he teaches Theology at Princeton University, and his sister is the President of a college in Seoul.

When Sang's mother died, Julia called almost immediately and told him that she saw his mother in Purgatory and urged him to quickly have Masses said for her soul. Almost a year later, Julia told Sang she saw his mother in Heaven.

When we left the church, Sang forgot to release the handbrake and after maybe five miles, the odor was quite strong. Heasook said, “Be sure you write about this, too.”

In both Koreas, and in Japan, China, and Russia, the abortion rate is higher than in the West. In all these countries, more than 50% of pregnancies end in abortions, compared with about 25% in the United States and 16% in Canada. Most people do not know clearly that the baby in the womb is a human being. They also have a strong social and economic pressure—always so busy to make money for survival and for advancement.

The Buddhist thinking that people become born again after death may also have contributed to the easy killings of the unborn babies. The Church in Korea says that abortion is wrong, but does not lead any vigorous fight against it.

We again discussed the chastisements when we were driving back home. Sang has a somewhat different feeling, and said he feels everything depends on what people do after the Warning. He feels the people will determine what happens. He said 2/3 to 3/4 will die, but no one knows. He feels the people will determine the number who die by the number who do not convert.

I told him about the building being built for food storage with three-foot walls. Sang said, "Convert and consecrate yourself to the Sacred Heart and to the Immaculate Heart. That is how you beat the chastisements."

Lunch today consisted of potato pasta with tomatoes, turkey, ham, and salad. It was a great meal. Our dinner was Kimakee, seaweed, tofu, bulgagi (beef sirloin in soy sauce), Galbi (beef short ribs in soy sauce), and rice. It was a Korean meal, but not too bad.

Heasook tries so hard to be a gracious hostess, and she is succeeding.

The next day we are to leave for Korea. We went to 8:00 a.m. Mass at St. Henry—opposite of Holy Rosary. We had breakfast at 8:45 a.m., and left for the airport at 10:15 a.m. The day was very difficult. It lasted 24 1/2 hours.

My observations are these: Korean people are a very worldly people. They are proud of their personal appearance. They are self confident, well educated, and in a great hurry. The women are wearing dresses or dress suits. Slacks are worn by less than 10% of the women. All of them, it seems, have great shapes. Almost zero are overweight. This is a good-looking race of people. The men are dressed to kill. Almost all are in suits, and almost all suits are black. Their hair is neat and trimmed. I saw no long hair and no jeans.

Everyone, it seems, has a mission. In my opinion—hurry, find a mate, have a family, make a bunch of money. Religion is way down on the list. Divorce is not like in the United States, because they put a higher value on family life, but that is beginning to change also.

We have a two-hour wait at the airport in Seoul before we can go to Kwangju. I had such a good time with Heasook. She, at one time, said, "That girl just got married today." I said, "How can you tell?" She said, "You tell by the hair and the makeup. Saturday is a big day for weddings and the gate we are observing is a flight to Chesju Island. This is a traditional place for honeymoon."

Sang said, "Korean people and Japanese people are group people. What some do, all do, almost all follow. That is why, in Korea, when Bishop is modern, priests follow and all the people follow. This is why, when conversions begin, the masses of the population will convert."

I mentioned to Heasook, "There are many pretty women in Korea. No fat girls, like me and others in the U.S." We came to the conclusion that this is because of their diet. They don't like milk or milk products, or bread, or potatoes.

We kept watching, and I said, "Here comes another bride, and another, and another, and soon a steady stream." Heasook said, "They all get their hair and makeup done at the beauty shop. That is why they all look the same." I told Heasook, "I vote they keep it this way. Women like trophies and men in their finest."

The call to start boarding the flight to Chesju Island was announced. Bang, all the couples lined up. I estimated there were close to 100 couples. Heasook said, "This is like being at a movie." I was amused. I walked up front and took some pictures. I think their reaction was like this: "This American finds us humorous; others gave the impression I was intruding; others were unconcerned... we have this job to do...serious business...get on with it."

But it was a tough day, though. At one point, I thought I was getting a signal. I said, "Hey, this is still early in the trip." Then I realized immediately, I thought Our Lady informed me, "I will take care of you. I do not want you to worry. I did not say I do not want you to suffer." That is what I felt, and then I was totally at peace. No more worry.

The next day was October 18. Notice, we missed a day. It was because of passing over the International Date Line.

Many years ago, there were three kingdoms in what is now South Korea. The SE conquered the SW and they then conquered the North and they became one. The SE was deprived politically and economically. Thus, for many it was a place of exile, very poor. Naju is here. This has changed somewhat. Well, everything changes.

Last November, the smell of Korean food was very, very offensive. It was a strong smell like a combination of garlic, spoiled fish, and boar meat. When I had arrived at Sang's house, there it was again. Now, here in Korea, it is the same odor, but it doesn't seem to be quite as bad. Could it be, if I stay too long, I could get to like it?

We went to Mass today in Kwangju...population 1 million. The population in Naju is 80,000. The church we went to is pro-Naju. After Mass, we went to Naju. What a simple little place. What was once a church is now a house of prayer. The Blessed Sacrament is not allowed, the tabernacle was removed, so was the altar, the pews, and the kneelers. No Mass is allowed, all by the orders of the Bishop.

Just about an empty building. It is no big deal. Koreans like to sit on the floor, anyway. There are no organized services. About 50 to 75 people were there from the U.S. No numbers like at Medjugorje, but something very powerful. Julia was in the hospital in Kwangju.

It is like Medjugorje without the visionaries. But then, the visionaries are not Medjugorje, and Julia is not Naju. I was told Julia is too sick to welcome the pilgrims, but Sang and I will be taken to see her. I told Sang I should not go, because I am no better than any other pilgrim. "So you go. I'll remain," I said. But, Sang said, "You are with me and you have no choice."

The next day, October 19, was the anniversary of the shedding of tears of blood. We were taken to the hospital at 9:30 a.m. to see Julia in Room 603. Father Chang and Father Seo were there, and now Sang, Heasook, and I.

I do not know any words to describe my feelings. To me, Julia is the most loving, affectionate, compassionate person, and we visited for some time, having volunteers preparing persimmon, pears, grapes, watermelon, and chestnuts.

After a while, I was told that she wants me to come closer to her so she could pray for me, because she wants my health to improve. Now she took my left hand and pulled it under the covers to herself and prayed out loud and also in song—hymns—for about five minutes, I would guess.

She squeezed my hand firmly, and when she finally released it and I pulled my hand back from underneath her covers, a strong beautiful fragrance came with my hand, the same as on the replica statue, and now it is on my hand. I was not told this could happen. I don't know if this happens always, sometimes, or seldom. No one told me. Our visit that day lasted three hours.

Father Chang wanted to take us to a fine Japanese restaurant but, wouldn't you know, we landed in a genuine authentic Korean restaurant. We were joined by two volunteers of Julia: Albino and Raphael. Raphael speaks good English. He is a tease and very funny. I met him in Los Angeles last November.

The table is 12 inches off the floor with three built-in burners. Albino cooked the pork, and Raphael the beef. Also, we had Kimchee, rice, chestnuts, and a bowl of garlic. The meat had no seasoning. You were supposed to dip the meat in any of four bowls which made it taste many times worse, but they all thought it was wonderful.

They brought a chair for me and everyone else sat on the floor. They laughed about it. They thought it made me look like the king, like Yul Brenner in "The King and I." Raphael was my closest subject, and also my favorite subject.

Raphael told about how Koreans discovered a part of the frog was very tasty—the legs—but they were too tiny, so they imported the large frog from the U.S. Problem was, the imported frogs ate all the Korean frogs, and when they finished off all the little frogs, the flies and mosquitoes took over the nation. Raphael and I thought this very humorous.

The rest didn't understand English. Raphael also told about the squirrels being much too small, so they imported this black squirrel, thinking they would get even bigger than normal because of the abundance of chestnuts. The black squirrels didn't like the chestnuts and wouldn't eat them and, desperate for food, they ate the Korean squirrels since they had no other food. The Koreans cook chestnuts like we cook potatoes.

Finally, I asked for sugar and milk. I showed them how to eat rice my way, but I don't think they were impressed. This was a fun, fun meal. Raphael, Albino, Fr. Chang, Fr. Seo, Sang, and Heasook are a super group of very devout traditional supporters of the Faith and of Julia. I am sure that Fr. Chang and I have found a bonded friendship. Fr. Chang has been sort of sent into exile because of his support of Julia, but even more because of his refusal to accept the modern movement of the Korean Church. I think the Korean Church may be worse than the American. In America, these modern Bishops pretend to support the Pope. In Korea, they openly deny his authority.

Later that day, we went to Naju to the chapel and remained there for the all-night prayer vigil, which lasted until 6 in the morning. The chapel was filled. I estimated there were about 500 people. I tried to count the rows. People were also outside where there were loudspeakers and TV monitors. I think this was a very difficult but rewarding experience.

The high point of this day was the intimate experience with Julia. I feel her health is worse than mine, yet her concern is for me. However, I also feel her health is in direct control by Our Lord, and she cannot pass on until He allows it, and I don't see how that can happen now. Of course, the same thing is true for everyone, but I can see it plainer in her.

It is the 20th of October, and today we go to the mountain where Bishop Danylak gave Communion to Julia that turned into the beating Heart of Jesus. Fr. Chang concelebrated that Mass. He had come also, and afterwards we went to chapel again, and then to the local church in Naju for 5 p.m. Mass, celebrated by Fr. Seo.

After that, Sang said, "I will take you to Julia's house. She will not be there, of course, but you can go there to rest at any time." After a minute or so in the house, to my surprise and also Sang's and Heasook's, in walked Julia from the other room. Julia had a look and a smile like, "I got you!"

Julia had been given permission to go home for a few hours. She sat on a flat pillow on the floor. There was no carpet, or linoleum. It was slick from the pillows and stocking feet. No one wore shoes in the house, though they said it was OK for me, but I was happy to take my shoes off.

I sat on a sofa, low to the floor. Fr. Chang sat to my right and Fr. Seo sat to my left. Everyone else sat on the floor. People came one at a time, as news spread that Julia was home. I counted 23 in the circle visiting. After a while, Fr. Chang got up and blessed several people...first Julia.

He blessed with fragrant oil from Julia's statue. This had formed into a solid substance and looked like make-up. I think this oil had been saved from a couple of years ago, yet it still had the fragrance. Father anointed the forehead, lips, eyes, ears, and chest. After Fr. Chang finished, Julia started praying and everyone joined hands.

She prayed, probably 15 minutes, out loud. She cried profusely. So did many others, as a reaction to her tears. Then she prayed over each one individually and, as she finished with each, they left until there were only about seven of us left. She would scoot on the floor on her pillow to each individual to pray over them.

I thought, maybe not me, because I can't get on the floor like the others. Then she looked at me with an affectionate smile, and came toward me. She came between my knees and put both arms around me, and rested her head on my chest. Without a doubt, this was the most emotional experience I have ever had, and could only be exceeded by Our Lady.

Now I am in tears, and she just smiles. We exchange, "I love you," and embrace another minute. I am positive she knows my feelings for her, my respect for the relationship she has with Our Lady, and my feelings of compassion for her sufferings and persecution. She is a true victim soul, a stigmatist and many other things. The lump was high in my throat. Today will be a day to remember, a day of emotional exhaustion.

I noticed that many, no maybe only some, are looking for the sensational signs, like the sun, etc. But, those close to Julia know the meaning and purpose of the messages from Our Lady.

On October 21, we went to Mass at 7:30 a.m., and then left for the hospital at 9:30 a.m. to visit with Julia for the last time. Two hours only, then we have to leave for the airport and fly to Seoul. At her room are Raphael, Albino, Sang, Heasook, and myself. Julia spoke Korean so Raphael or Sang would interpret. Julia said at one point, "Do all you can to avoid or bypass Purgatory. The suffering is physical, mental, and emotional. Much of Purgatory is red like fire, but no flames."

She was made to see lay people, religious, priests, bishops, cardinals, but was also unable to identify them. She spent 3 1/2 hours in Purgatory by choice to offer her suffering. She said one hour is like years. Hell is much worse. In Hell, the flames are high and the people are tossed like sparks in a fireplace. Julia only passed through Hell, but did not suffer there. She had also been to Heaven more than once and experienced death more than once.

She then showered us with fruit...pears, melon, persimmon, and chestnuts. Then, many gifts. Then, she prayed over Sang, Heasook, and myself. She is what no words can describe. My feelings are also that I can find no words for my intimate emotional experience. I try to hold on to this moment. It is difficult to give it up. I think she has a one-on-one relationship with each person, though each one is different.

We then left for Seoul. I will always remember how trivial are the things of this world. We arrived in Seoul at 6:30 p.m., and were met by Sang's sister and her husband, Dr. Kim, and his older brother Rev. S. H. Lee. They took us to dinner.

On October 22, we went to Mass at 6:30 a.m. at the Cathedral, a ten-minute walk from the hotel. Sang called Fr. Spies after Mass, and we went there via the subway which took about 2 hours. A young lady there prepared a big meal, Korean, for Fr. Spies and Sang, and herself...and German for me, bless her heart.

Fr. Spies is older than I am, close to 80, and still a pastor of a church. He is half French, half German...a Salesian missionary priest from France...a very humble and most kind priest...very much involved with Julia. He collects and sends all the information, pictures, and documents regarding Julia to the Vatican. He has a mountain of documents on his desk.

He has a small chapel where he has exposed the Eucharist which came from Heaven during two of the seven Eucharistic miracles of Hosts coming down. Fr. Spies is not just any ordinary priest. He is pictured and quoted all over in books, newspapers, and publication. Meeting him is like meeting a great celebrity after reading and seeing articles about him for a number of years.

Another remarkable day...seeing the Hosts exposed, and having dinner in his home. And, this young girl who works for Father is another remarkable person. She is both secretary and cook. I asked, "Do you live here?"

"Yes," she answered.

I remarked to her, "It is unbelievable to see such a pretty and youthful girl living and taking care of such an aged priest." She replied, "This is my vocation. I feel blessed, honored, and privileged." She has given her life. I guessed her age at 24, but was later told she has worked for Fr. Spies for 16 years.

She then walked us to a cabstand for the ride back to the subway. We arrived back at the hotel and were supposed to go to dinner with Justin Park. He publishes the *Catholic Digest*, and has written about being present at a Eucharistic miracle.

I begged off, because the subway journey was all I could handle. It was 133 steps down, and it is like another city down there. Shop after shop, like a giant mall. Tonight, I felt like it was my first day of a two-a-day football practice.

This is the end of the pilgrimage. Tomorrow, we go back to the United States.

Above: Father Su and George meet again in Korea
Below: Dinner with friends in Korean restaurant

Above: Sang Lee and Julia Kim in Julia's home
Below: George visits Julia in a hospital in Korea

Above: George and Fr. Spies at Fr. Spies' chapel.
George holds replica of Julia Kim's statue of miracles,
and Fr. Spies holds one of the Eucharistic miracles
Below: George, Fr. Spies, and Sang Lee at Fr. Spies' home

Chapter 13

Statue of Our Lady in India

I was told that two particular situations took place in India at two locations, two to three hours apart. Both had received replica statues. With each statue...pictures, videos, and reading material were included, in order that what was going on in Naju by the Blessed Mother, through Julia Kim, would become known. The messages of Our Blessed Mother are what are so important.

Following are some excerpts from Father Garfield Jansen's letters from Coimbatore, India:

"I love the apparitions at Naju and am spreading them in India. I am very grateful for the statue. Thank you once again. I love it very, very, very much. It will have a special place of honor and veneration here. God bless and reward you abundantly with peace and grace. I place you in the patronage and arms of Mary. She loves you very much and cares for you. Be assured always of my friendship and my support. Do not worry. You are Mary's unique person and God's gift to us. You make us so happy.

"Please find enclosed packets of cloth absorbed in the myrrh perfume tears of Mary. I hope you like this precious gift. The tears are coming from the two pictures of Mary that you sent to us. It is flowing continuously. The statue, too, has started to bleed.

"Thousands of people are coming from all parts of India to see the statue and the pictures. Even Archbishops come. Please see the enclosed photos. The fruits are wonderful—there have been so many conversions, cures, miracles, etc. We are so happy. Credit goes to Mary. We love Mary very much. Please help us. I trust in you.

"The faith of the people is increasing, and they live holier and more charitable lives.

"P.S.—You must see the joy and happiness of the faces of those who gaze on the pictures of Mary shedding tears of perfume, and the statue of Mary shedding blood. Mary is with you. I will always help you, and be your friend. Father Jensen."

"I want to become a saint and do good to all humanity, and end the pain and suffering in the world. This is my only aim. Father Jensen."

I was informed that an area was in great need of a church. They wanted help. They asked, "Would you help?" I answered, "Sure, but in return, will you help? If you get a new church, will you place the statue of Our Lady from Naju in a place of honor, and inform your people about the messages through Julia Kim so they can venerate and receive Our Lady's special graces?" This was a great trade-off, and formed a solid relationship.

Below are excerpts from a letter from the pastor of St. Mary's Church in Karnataka, India: (Imagine my pleasant surprise when I saw the name of this parish.):

"I am joyful and overwhelmed to receive the statue of Our Lady of Naju, Korea and the messages received by Julia Kim, and also I received a video cassette. The statue reached me safely. I watched the cassette, and it must have been a wonderful experience in Julia Kim's life. May God be glorified.

"On the 29th, we will be having a special Mass in honor of Blessed Mother and in the sermon, Julia Kim's life and the wonders of the Lord in her life will be preached, so that our people may be drawn more closely to the Eucharistic Lord. Once the new church is completed, this statue will be placed with due honor by our Bishop.

"The church work is in progress and now it has reached the roof level. We are getting ready to put on the roof slab. Since the rains are continuing, the work is slow. It may take another two months to complete the roof slab. Once the roof slab is casted, I shall send you the photos. This church is going to be a beautiful house of God.

"I really admire your faith and devotion. Your life has been an instrument for my priestly ministry. From the first day of my priesthood to this date, my motto is: 'Hope and Love all in Christ.'

"I request you to enroll my parish for the 'Mary's Touch By Mail,' so that we, too, may get the messages and share them among us.

"I need your constant prayers to complete the task that has been entrusted to me by the Lord to build His house. Please remember me in your prayers."

Another letter: "We had the solemn installation of the statue of Our Lady, who draws us to the Eucharist. I was the main celebrant, and with me, five priests from my deanery concelebrated the Holy Mass. During the sermon, a Capuchin priest explained the mysteries of the Body and Blood of Christ, and how our Blessed Mother worked wonders in the life of Julia. The liturgy was lovely. After the Holy Communion, the statue was blessed and installed inside the wooden niche prepared by one of our youth.

"Every Monday is dedicated to Our Lady of the Eucharist. We will have one hour of adoration followed by the Holy Mass, every first Monday of the month. We will have 7 a.m. to 12 noon exposition of the Blessed Sacrament, and in the evening, Mass of Our Lady of the Eucharist will be celebrated. Please continue to pray that this devotion and piety may increase in my parish and spread throughout the diocese."

Another letter: "Dear Mr. George. One thing that I long for my people, wherever I work, is that they show great reverence, and receive the Body and Blood of Christ with due honor and respect. Now I am satisfied, for the Mother is going to be with me and my people to draw us more closely to the Eucharistic Lord. Please do send me the messages of Our Lady of Naju regularly, for they will be useful for my sermons.

"My younger brother is in the Jesuit order. His ordination is on November 19, 1999. It would be nice if you could make a trip to India and join in the celebration. It will be chilly, and nice weather. His name is P. R. John. Please pray for him in your daily prayers.

"My parish consists of 18 mission stations, with a radius of about 40 to 50 kilometers. In these mission stations, Catholic children's faith, as well as their education, is zero. In order to strengthen their faith and raise up their standard of education, I have started a home on the church premises. There are about 35 children. They are doing well. All these children's parents are daily wagers. Life in their villages is miserable, yet they are devout people. May God bless them.

"Thank you very much for your concern and your generosity to know my needs. I shall let you know in my next letter. May Blessed Mother guide and give you good health."

Father Paulraj has stayed in contact about weekly, and kept me informed of the progress. He showed his gratefulness to me often, but I feel that my part was not so much a gift to them as it was a gift to me from Our Lady. I think it is almost necessary to be in my shoes to understand this.

In any event, I know this was a huge culmination of two years of labor by many people who labored for $1.00 per day. They made the sacrifice, and I am so happy for them. I kept thinking, as this was being built, it cannot amount to much. I saw the bamboo scaffolding used and what amounted to human elevators. The final product is a beautiful church worthy to be called St. Mary's. The beauty shocked me.

The dedication was held on March 23, 2000, and what a celebration! I think the special Mass and Blessing lasted five hours, according to a note from Father Paulraj: "March 23 was a big feast and blessing day for the whole town of Manvi. From all religions, people partook in the celebration to get God's blessings. Even today, this is the talk of the town. Over 7000 people attended the Blessing and partook in common meal. You were always in my heart."

And, on March 23, Father Paulraj called me at 10:30 p.m. India's time, to express his excitement, and he told me the church is dedicated to the destitute children, and that the Bishop blessed a special destitute child who represented all the destitute. Her name is "Yellemma."

I asked him, "What is a destitute child?" He told me that she has no one. I said, "You mean an orphan?"

"No," he replied. "She has no parents, no family, no home, no one to care for her." I asked, "Who will take care of her?" Father Paulraj replied, "I will." He told me she is a little Hindu.

I kept inquiring about this little girl each time we talked together. Father told me, after about six weeks, “This little girl has attended Mass every day, on her own, and is taking instructions.” This again makes me feel totally rewarded, and the following pictures tell it all.

Above: The Bishop blessed Yellemma, a little Hindu girl, who represented the destitute children

Above: Pictures of the statue sent to Fr. Jansen shedding tears

Below: Fr. Garfield Jansen holding picture of replica statue shedding tears

St. Mary's Church in India under construction

Above, left: Place of honor for Julia Kim's replica statue at St. Mary's Church, India. Above, right: Fr. Paulraj
Below: Fr. Paulraj, Pastor of St. Mary's Church in India on the Day of Dedication

Above: Every priest of the diocese was present at the Dedication of St. Mary's Church

Below: Crowd at Dedication of St. Mary's Church 7000 stayed for meal after the Dedication

St. Mary's Church on the Day of Dedication

Completed St. Mary's Church by day and night

Chapter 14

Meeting Annemaria

On the morning of September 3, 1999, about 11:00 a.m., I first met Annemaria Schmidt, as she entered the dining area of a convent. I was sitting on a desk chair, bent down searching for a key to unlock the roll top, when I heard the door open behind me. Looking back over my shoulder, seeing her, I said, “Oh, I know who you are.” She replied, “And I know who you are, too, Mr. George.” She paused just a moment and then added, “I've been praying for you for a long time. I asked the Blessed Mother to please let me meet you, and now She has answered my prayers.”

I couldn't find words to respond. I recognized her from a video I saw, but could not understand how she knew to pray for me. I needed to find out. I asked her if I could speak to her at some length later, and she agreed.

We spoke all Friday afternoon, as the retreat that she was conducting didn't start until 7 p.m. I had not planned on making the retreat. This was not my purpose. This was, however, one of my best retreats. I know now that meeting this lady was a planned meeting. I have never, at any time, had a difference of opinion with this person.

We have become very good friends, and even though she lives a great distance away, we have become even better friends through long-distance phone conversations. It is a great privilege to call on her for guidance at any time. We spoke after most conferences, and then again all Sunday afternoon after the retreat was over.

We discussed Father Malachi Martin, a friend of hers. We discussed Fr. Gobbi, whose interpreter is also a friend of hers. At one point, I asked her, "Do you know Pope John II?" She said, "Yes." I said, "OK, but does John Paul II know you?" She smiled and answered "Yes. He often came to our lodge to ski." I asked, "Where was this?" She said, "Czechoslovakia."

We spoke about everything I could think of, and she was very candid. I would never betray her confidence. We discussed Pope John XXIII, Garabandal, Medjugorje, Julia Kim, Pius X group, Archbishop Lefebvre, Fatima, the third secret, consecration of Russia, Father Gruner, and Father Fox.

I then asked her, "What kind of perfume or cologne do you use?" She said, "I don't use any, why?" I said, "A fragrance comes from you. This is the second time I noticed it. The first time was when you sat down beside me in the chapel and I recognized the fragrance is the same as Julia Kim."

She said, "I am told that sometimes, but not often. I am not aware of it." I then asked, "Has Russia been consecrated as requested by Our Lady at Fatima?" Her answer confirmed my suspicions.

Now I asked her, "Who was your father?" She replied, "He was a baron." I said, "I don't know what that is." She said, "He was the richest man in Czechoslovakia. He owned factories and businesses all over the nation, and was the nation's largest employer...and he was an outstanding Catholic."

I said, "I knew a man who escaped from behind the Iron Curtain from Czechoslovakia. He employed 400. He told me the government nationalized everything, starting with the biggest on down." She said, "Yes, my father was first." I asked, "What happened?" And, she said, "He was shot. So was my mother, and so was my brother."

I asked how she had escaped, and she told me that she was away at Medical College in Prague at the time. She continued, "One day, a truck pulled up at the school, and some of us were loaded in the back and taken to Auschwitz. They took us there for brainwashing...and daily beatings were part of it, but they could not brainwash me because I fought it, and my faith was too strong. One day 75 of us were facing the firing squad... 74 died. They missed me. How could they miss me?"

I said, "I guess someone else was involved." She said, "Someone else is always involved. When the war was going badly on the Eastern Front, and also in Africa, the Germans needed cannon fodder." I asked her, "What is cannon fodder?" She said, "It is when they put you in the line of almost certain death.

"They took men previously captured and forced them to fight the Russians, and I was selected to go along as a medical doctor, even though I was not qualified. They didn't care. I was forced to perform surgeries without any facilities, out in the open, and the screaming I heard gives me flashbacks yet today. I had no training for any of this."

She continued, "Eventually we were captured, and I was sent to Siberia to a Russian concentration camp. I learned to speak German even though I hated it, but my father told me it could help me later. This is why I was not shot at Auschwitz. They needed me.

"Now I decided to learn Russian, and that, too, later became helpful. I was placed in a small cell, cold and dark, and I thought I had the meanest guard. I thought he was the meanest man in the world. He raped and killed two women every week. He beat me daily, and one day he beat me so badly, I was down on the ground and I was certain I was dying. I looked up at him, and said, 'I forgive you, and Jesus forgives you, too.'

"He wanted to know Who Jesus was. He thought He was my boyfriend. I told him, and he came to my cell every night for over a month, and I told him Bible stories. Finally, one night, he looked at my Crucifix and asked, 'This Jesus you call the Savior, could He love me, too?'

"I told him that he must be baptized. He asked me to baptize him, and I said that it must be done by a priest. He poked his rifle into my ribs and said, 'You do it.' I thought if I could get him to the river, I could push him in and he would get under some ice, and no one would ever see him again.

"We went to the river and I told him to put down his rifle but he refused. I insisted I would not baptize him if he didn't put down his rifle; so, reluctantly, he did. When I had my chance I pushed him, but I didn't know he had his two hands gripped on to my coat, and when he went in, he pulled me in with him...so, I baptized him."

"Then we climbed out of the river and we were like two blocks of ice. Our clothes quickly froze, and he took me with him to the Commandant's office to warm and dry off. The Commandant soon learned that I spoke both German and Russian, and he decided I now belonged to him.

"He was the ugliest man I ever saw. He was from Mongolia, very short, with very bowed legs from riding ponies a lot when he was young...and he had long hair coming down both sides of his chin. He informed me that if I didn't do as he asked, he would chop off my fingers, then my feet, then my head. I told him that would be fine! Then I wouldn't have to work any longer for him.

"Meanwhile, the meanest guard became a gentle giant. He was 6' 4", and now he was very respectful of women. He became the total opposite of what he was before. I thank God that through all of this, I had never been raped.

"I had been in this camp for 18 months, and the war was coming to a close. Russia was preparing to return some of the prisoners in this concentration camp. I was one of the last to arrive.

"They loaded a boxcar with 80 prisoners. I was in this first group to leave because this gentle guard gave me a shawl and tag #9, and lifted me and pushed me into the boxcar and closed the door. The woman who had tag #9 had died the previous night, and he took her shawl and tag and placed them on me.

"Now the car began to move. There was one barrel of water on the boxcar and I had enough medical knowledge to know I had to drink the water. By the second day, some were coming down with cholera. As people died, they were stacked at one end of the boxcar.

"The last thing the Russians did was push the boxcar into the American zone. During the two weeks of travel, 78 of the 80 of us died. The smell was very bad. The Americans came close to getting rid of the problem by using flame throwers, but one man insisted someone could be alive. So, wearing gas masks and protective clothing, this one man and a nurse came in and found me unconscious. They carried me and one other person off, and I woke up in a hospital with a nun sitting at my bedside."

What a great lady! She speaks five languages that I know of. I would not be surprised if she spoke ten. The similarities with Julia Kim are many. We then discussed the future of the world, the nation, and the Church. Not a rosy outlook!

Annemaria is a true close friend. She is someone I can call on when I need counsel. I have deep feelings for this lady, and I consider her a gift from Our Blessed Lady. I call her when I have a question. I call her when I need someone to talk with. I admire her so very much. I feel rewarded, and, when I die, I want to be where she is.

Above: Annemaria...Below: Annemaria and George

Chapter 15

Divine Mercy Messenger

One day, in the second half of the year 2000, I received a call from Tim McAndrew, the editor of *The Divine Mercy Messenger.* As usual, he was given false information about me, and the only thing correct was my phone number. He lives and works out of central Ohio.

He asked if he could send a couple of previous issues, which, on receiving, I thought were quite good. He then printed a new issue, which dealt with plenary indulgences for the Poor Souls gained by going through certain Holy Doors, designated by the Bishop of a diocese, and also meeting the other requirements set up by the Holy See.

I knew this was not new, but to me it was an awakening. I didn't feel it was emphasized anywhere as much as it was in this paper. What happened, proved that many of our lay people and certain of our clergy felt the same way.

I was asked to take 500 copies. I said OK, but ended up with 3000! Then one lady I had contacted in Omaha asked for 6000, and then more. This lady personally made the contacts, got permission, and then placed them...a giant task. Sometimes the hardest job was getting permission to exhibit the papers.

I know our lay people are underestimated. Some places we were told 25 would be enough, but then they used several hundred. Two pastors asked for 1000 immediately. Word of mouth did it all. Some 17,000 went through my office alone. Copies were mailed to Florida, Louisiana, Kansas, Nebraska, Illinois, Missouri, Alabama, Arizona, Iowa, and many other places.

Numbers were not the goal, and areas were not either. I had no plan. This thing just took off. It is still ongoing, and the editor accuses me of his problem. He had only distributed them in his own diocese and now they are in demand throughout much of the United States.

The editor of this newspaper has become a good friend, and he and three others took a flight to Dubuque to attend an apparition with Ivan. I thought it was a sizable sacrifice. However, he said, "It's a lot closer than Medjugorje."

Now, two years later, the *Divine Mercy Messenger* is stronger than ever, and Tim keeps telling me that he doesn't really know what he is doing. I think this is why Our Blessed Mother uses him. If he were capable, he would be with some big publishing company. This contact, like several others, is a joy in my life.

Chapter 16

Mary With Me

Dearest Mother Mary, I want to address this final chapter publicly and directly to You. How does one address the Mother of my Lord? I don't know. I have always called Your attention just by "Hey Mary." I don't know the flowing words. I know my prayer would never be printed. I would not be putting together what is in these previous pages if I didn't think You wanted them assembled. If it helps one person, my efforts are rewarded. You have put many people in my path, and I consider them all gifts from You.

You are, right now, placing a lump in my throat so big and so heavy I cannot swallow, and the tears make it difficult to see the paper before me. You have done this many times—through Ivan, Julia Kim, Father Paulraj, Annemaria—I cannot name them all.

This book is not a diary of my entire life. These pages are only about the last dozen years, when You changed my focus from here to eternity. I will be eternally grateful. I know that I am not capable of doing this on my own. I don't feel capable of anything anymore, without You. You know, in the past, I thought I was in control. I felt I could do certain things, but I have learned that somebody was lurking in the shadows watching all my errors and worldly endeavors. You made me see Your presence in my journey, which I think is also in the final chapter.

I am not capable of doing for You what You deserve. I just hope You continue to make me see Your presence, because I need You now more than ever. I hope You will remain first in my life for the remaining days. I know You haven't singled me out, but sometimes I feel a little bit spoiled. I think everyone needs to feel this way. Thank You for everything.